THE
IN THE WHERE
THEY WERE BORN

IN THE TOWN WHERE THEY WERE BORN

Smirnoff
the original Vodka
DOUBLE DIAMOND

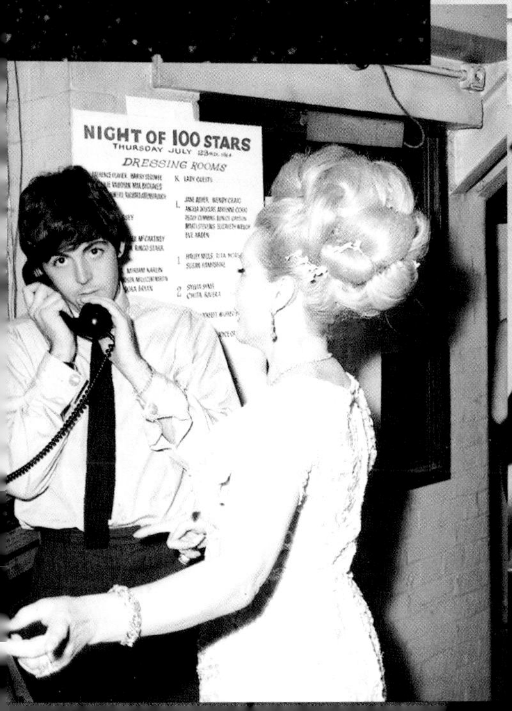
NIGHT OF 100 STARS
THURSDAY JULY
DRESSING ROOMS

THE

HIT
RINGO
STARR

ACKNOWLEDGEMENTS

I would like to thank my world, Julie, for her patience, understanding and love over the past several years whilst researching for this book.

Also our daughter, Kathryn, and our two sons, Robert and Michael, for their support, trust and for always believing this would become reality one day.

My dearest friends Allan and Jane Pickersgill who have travelled this journey with me and my family, and given me such inspiration to continue.

I am very grateful to my work colleagues for their support, especially David Stoker, Ruth Hobbins and Roger Hull. My gratitude to Paul and Mike McCartney and all the McCartney family and I hope you enjoy this nostalgic trip down your family memory lane.

I am indebted to a number of people who have given me invaluable assistance in the researching and writing of this book. They are Graham and Julie Hodson, for Graham's meticulous research on Liverpool at War. Kevin Martin, a Liverpool Institute old boy. Ray O'Brien, Beatles historian and Liverpool Institute old boy. Professor Iain C Taylor, MA, PHD (chief geographer, Government of Canada, retired) and Liverpool Institute old boy. Mark Lewisohn, Beatles historian. The Liverpool Record Office for their archived resources. Ken Rogers, Alan Jewell, Jamie Dunmore and Lee Ashun from Trinity Mirror and finally Miss Anne Edis, the first person to proof-read this book.

Dedication: I will be forever in the debt of those I love and miss greatly but I know are looking down on me with pride. God bless the Foley and Roach families and the Foster and Smyth families.

'Thanks Nellie' KEVIN ROACH

Trinity Mirror NW²

In The Town Where They Were Born Editor: Alan Jewell **Design:** Jamie Dunmore
Sub Editors: Michael Haydock and Peter Grant
Executive Editor: Ken Rogers **Senior Editor:** Steve Hanrahan **Senior Art Editor:** Rick Cooke **Senior Production Editor:** Paul Dove
Writers: Chris McLoughlin, David Randles, Gavin Kirk, William Hughes, John Hynes, Simon Hughes
Design Team: Barry Parker, Colin Sumpter, Glen Hind, Alison Gilliland, James Kenyon, Lisa Critchley
Photography: Trinity Mirror, Paul and Michael McCartney, Liverpool Record Office, PA Photos, Lee Ashun, Mirrorpix
Printed by: Pensord
Sales & Marketing Manager: Elizabeth Morgan 0151 285 8412
Write to: Trinity Mirror, PO BOX 48, Liverpool L69 3EB

INTRODUCTION

Everyone has heard of Paul McCartney, one of four lads from Liverpool who shook the world.

However, not everyone knows about the people and places he'll remember all his life.

This book explores his past in unprecedented detail. It tells the story of his family background and influences, from the birth of his grandparents in the 19th century to the point where the Fab Four began to change popular music forever in the early 1960s.

Four years of painstaking research by Kevin Roach, of the Liverpool Record Office, has brought this story to life. We go on a nostalgic journey through the streets of Liverpool where the McCartney family grew up, and discover how those places have changed over the years.

This book takes you back to the days before 'Love Me Do' and 'Please Please Me', to a time of tramlines and cobblestones, gas mantles and open fires, air raids and pre-fab housing.

Paul (top left) and school friends stare in wonder at a replica of the crown jewels in Liverpool's Anglican Cathedral, 1952

With the Queen at the
Walker Art Gallery, July 2002

A ROYAL DISCOVERY

Here's a glimpse of the first piece of creative work by Paul McCartney that brought him to the attention of a wider public.

It's an essay Paul wrote, aged 10, to mark the coronation of Queen Elizabeth II in 1953.

As he was approaching the end of his research for this book, Kevin Roach discovered the essay, which had been lost within the vast archive of Liverpool Central Library for over 50 years.

Shortly before the coronation, it had been entered into a competition run by Liverpool's libraries and Paul's effort was a winner in his age-group category.

He was presented with a book token by Liverpool's Lord Mayor at an official ceremony in the city's Picton Library.

In neat handwriting, Paul displays an early fascination with the monarchy, referring to "the lovely, young Queen Elizabeth" and declaring that, "present day royalty rules with affection rather than force".

Within 12 years the Beatles would be awarded MBEs, although John Lennon returned his in 1969. In 1997 Paul became Sir Paul as he was knighted.

There are plenty of links between Paul McCartney and the Queen. In 1969 he wrote the song 'Her Majesty', which was the final (initially hidden) track on the 'Abbey Road' album.

In the classic Beatles' song 'Penny Lane', the fireman character carried a "portrait of the Queen" in his pocket.

When Paul helped establish the Liverpool Institute For Performing Arts (LIPA) on the site of his secondary school in 1996, it was the Queen who performed the official opening.

In June 2002 he performed in the gardens of Buckingham Palace to mark the Queen's golden jubilee. The following month they met again at the Walker Art Gallery in Liverpool as she toured an exhibition of Paul's paintings.

A complete reproduction of the essay and a transcript of the text can be found in chapter 7, on page 66

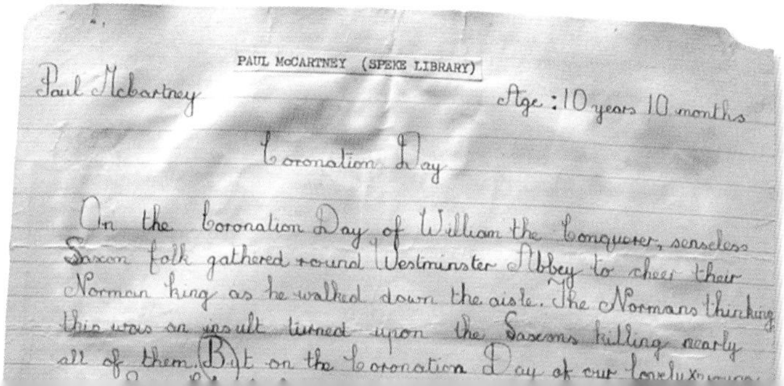

PAUL McCARTNEY (SPEKE LIBRARY)

Paul McCartney Age: 10 years 10 months

Coronation Day

On the Coronation Day of William the Conqueror, senseless Saxon folk gathered round Westminster Abbey to cheer their Norman king as he walked down the aisle. The Normans thinking this was an insult turned upon the Saxons killing nearly all of them. But on the Coronation Day of our

CONTENTS

Joe and Florrie married at Christ Church, Kensington, in 1896. The last service at the church took place in 1975. It is now used as a warehouse

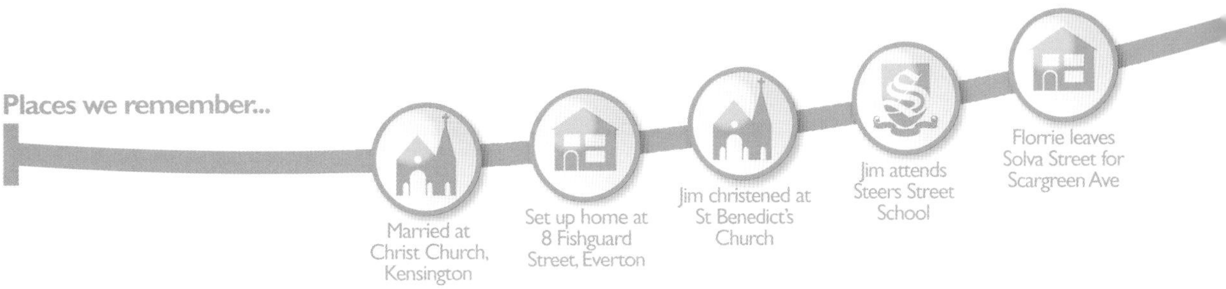

CHAPTER 1 THIS BOY

JOSEPH (JOE) MCCARTNEY AND FLORENCE (FLORRIE) CLEGG (PATERNAL GRANDPARENTS)

Paul McCartney's grandparents, Joe and Florrie, were both born in Liverpool and brought up in the densely populated terraced houses of Everton.

They were married at ***Christ Church, Kensington***, on May 17 1896. Joe, who was living on Wightman Street, had been engaged to another girl but soon had his head turned when Florrie moved nearby. Joe was 29 and Florrie 21 at the time of their wedding.

Shortly after marrying, Joe and Florrie moved to ***8 Fishguard Street, Everton***. After a few years they moved to Lloyd Street and then to Solva Street. They went on to have eight children, although two died young at a time when the infant mortality rate was very high.

Florrie was the loving and caring mum while Joe was the strict father. He worked all his life as a tobacco cutter, at Cope's tobacco firm, which was based in St Vincent Street, just off London Road.

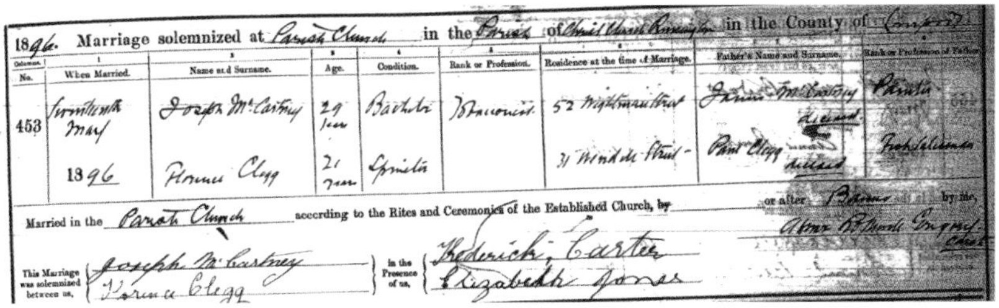

1896. Marriage solemnized at Parish Church in the Parish of Christ Church Kensington in the County of Lancaster

No.	When Married.	Name and Surname.	Age.	Condition.	Rank or Profession.	Residence at the time of Marriage.	Father's Name and Surname.	Rank or Profession of Father.
453	Seventeenth May 1896	Joseph McCartney	29 years	Bachelor	Tobacconist	52 Wightman Street	James McCartney	Painter
		Florence Clegg	21 years	Spinster		31 [illegible] Street	Paul Clegg	[illegible]

Married in the Parish Church according to the Rites and Ceremonies of the Established Church, by or after Banns by me,

This Marriage was solemnized between us, Joseph McCartney, Florence Clegg

in the Presence of us, Frederick Carter, Elizabeth Jones

Marriage lines of Joe McCartney and Florrie Clegg, Paul's grandparents

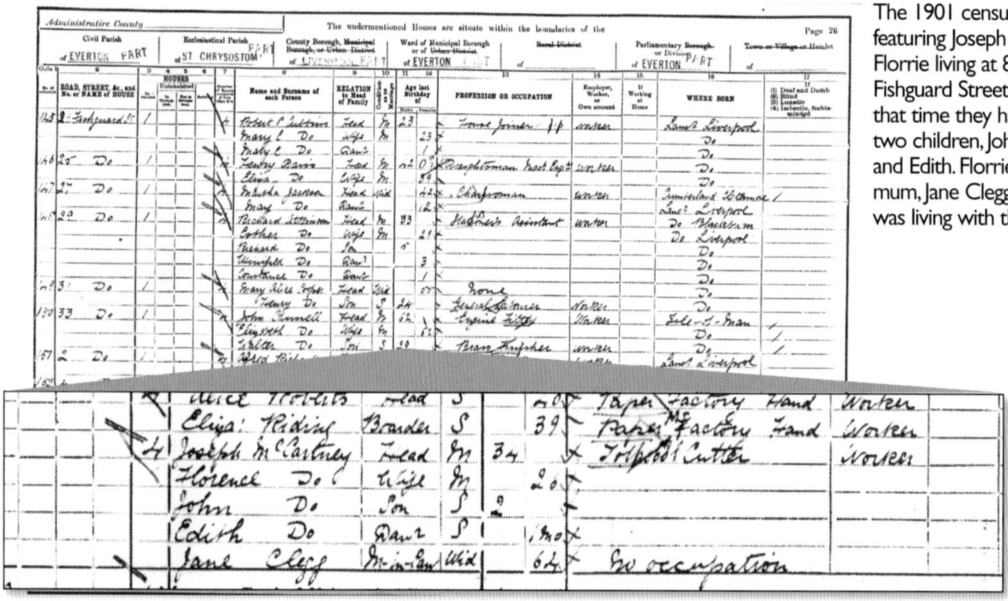

Administrative County

The undermentioned Houses are situate within the boundaries of the — Page 26

Civil Parish of EVERTON PART | Ecclesiastical Parish of ST CHRYSOSTOM PART | County Borough, ~~Municipal Borough, or Urban District~~ of LIVERPOOL PART | Ward of Municipal Borough or of ~~Urban District~~ of EVERTON PART | ~~Rural District~~ of | Parliamentary ~~Borough~~ or Division of EVERTON PART | ~~Town or Village or Hamlet~~ of

No. of Schedule	Road, Street, &c., and No. or Name of House	Name and Surname of each Person	Relation to Head of Family	Condition as to Marriage	Age (Males)	Age (Females)	Profession or Occupation	Employer, Worker, or Own account	Where Born	Infirmity
145	2 Fishguard St	Robert C Sutton	Head	M	23		House Joiner	Worker	Lanc Liverpool	
		Mary C Do	Wife	M		23			Do	
		Mary C Do	Daur			1			Do	
146	25 Do	Henry Davis	Head	M	62		Draughtsman Mach Eng	Worker	Do	
		Eliza Do	Wife	M		59			Do	
147	27 Do	Martha Jackson	Head	Wid		42	Charwoman	Worker	Cumberland [illegible]	/
		Mary Do	Daur			12			Lanc Liverpool	
148	29 Do	Richard Atkinson	Head	M	33		Hatter's Assistant	Worker	Do Blackburn	
		Esther Do	Wife	M		21			Do Liverpool	
		Richard Do	Son		5				Do	
		Winifred Do	Daur			3			Do	
		Constance Do	Daur			1			Do	
149	31 Do	Mary Alice Cooper	Head	Wid		55	None		Do	
		Henry Do	Son	S	24		General Labourer	Worker	Do	
150	33 Do	John Kennell	Head	M	62		Engine Fitter	Worker	Isle of Man	/
		Elizabeth Do	Wife	M		62			Do	/
		Walter Do	Son	S	29		Brass Finisher	Worker	Do	/
151	2 Do	Alfred Rich[illegible]						Worker	Lanc Liverpool	

Name and Surname of each Person	Relation to Head of Family	Condition as to Marriage	Age (Males)	Age (Females)	Profession or Occupation	Employer, Worker, or Own account
Alice Roberts	Head	S		40	Paper Factory Hand	Worker
Eliza Riding	Boarder	S		39	Paper Factory Hand	Worker
Joseph McCartney	Head	M	34		Tobacco Cutter	Worker
Florence Do	Wife	M		26		
John Do	Son	S	2			
Edith Do	Daur	S		1 mo		
Jane Clegg	M-in-Law	Wid		64	No occupation	

The 1901 census, featuring Joseph and Florrie living at 8 Fishguard Street. By that time they had two children, John and Edith. Florrie's mum, Jane Clegg, was living with them

Two images of Fishguard Street from the 1960s before the houses were demolished

Joe and Florrie moved to Lloyd Street from Fishguard Street

The junction of Wightman Street and Lloyd Street. Love blossomed between Paul's grandparents in this area

29 Lloyd Street in 1966

The junction of Breck Road and Breckfield Road South in October 2009. The furniture store building (blue exterior) was home to the Theatre Royal, where Jim McCartney worked as a boy. It was once also a cinema, as the sign indicates (opposite page)

Fishguard Close, off Breck Road. Modern houses in the area that was Fishguard Street, where the McCartneys lived at the turn of the 20th century

Lloyd Close (off Fishguard Close), looking towards the Everton water tower

Above: Cope's tobacco warehouse in 1966, shortly before it was demolished. Joe spent all his adult working life here

SOLVA ST.—E

15 *Hodson place*

LEFT SIDE.

1 Turner Isaac Slater boiler maker
3 McCartney Joseph operative tobcnst
5 Simnor William labourer
7 Ley Alexander engine fitter
9 Gibson Thomas Carter butcher
11 Kenagh Mrs. Antonetta
13 Hulme James labourer
15 Pierce John ship's steward
17 Peet George ironmonger's assistant
19 Ley Herbt. labourer
21 Ryan Miss Margaret
23 Simnor John Walter labourer
25 Lyons Dennis motor driver
27 Bonnett Mrs. Elizabeth
29 Caine William Louis plumber
31 Foy Herbert cotton porter
33 Rogers Mrs. Alice
35 Murphy Joseph french polisher
37 Hilton Edwin coal dealer
39 Davies James labourer
41 Bennett William cooper
43 Bell William labourer
45 Birkett Frederick pensioner
47 Jones Thomas John fruit selector

RIGHT SIDE.

2 Bird Arth. warehsmn
4 Gillespie Mrs. Georgina
6 Stephenson Ernest floor layer
8 Morris Mrs. Margaret
10 Harper Mrs. Maude
12 Knott Bertram labourer
14 Morris Mrs. Susan
16 Bushell James railwayman
18 Lappin Thomas tailor
20 Hatton Joseph George painter
22 Blundell John railway porter

Solva Street residents' directory. The McCartneys lived at number 3

While working at Cope's, Joe indulged his interest in music. He played in their brass band, as well as the Territorial Army's band. He also encouraged his children to play music, which the rest of the family enjoyed.

Joe's love of music was infectious and many a happy evening was spent with the neighbours of Solva Street, taking part in an impromptu concert in the street. Music was a means of escape from the poverty and despair of working-class Liverpool.

JAMES (JIM) MCCARTNEY

Paul's father, Jim, was born on July 7 1902. He was baptised two months after birth at ***St Benedict's Church of England chapel, Heyworth Street.***

Jim was educated at ***Steers Street School***, with the rest of the McCartney clan. It was two streets away from Solva Street. Aged around 10, he fell off a wall and permanently damaged his hearing. Whilst still at school, he became a programme seller and limelight boy for the Theatre Royal, Breck Road, Everton.

Everton Brow, 1927. On the right is the Roundhouse (also known as Prince Rupert's Tower), built in 1787 as a small lock-up. It was adopted by Everton Football Club for their official crest

Far left: A TA Church Parade in 1908 on Lime Street. Joe played in the TA brass band

Left: Everton, 1966

Paul's father, Jim, was born on July 7 1902. He was baptised two months after birth at St Benedict's Church of England chapel, Heyworth Street

THE

THEATRE ROYAL,

Breck Road, Everton, Liverpool.

PROPRIETOR - - - - MR. M. MONTGOMERY.
ACTING MANAGER - - - - MR. F. O'TOOLE.
STAGE MANAGER - - - - MR. FRED NEWBOLD.

POPULAR PRICES:—

Boxes,	Orchestra Stalls,	Circle,	Pit,
£1 1s. and 10/6 Single Seats, 2/-	1/6	1/-	6D.

If your Eyes are failing, purchase a Pair of

THOS. HOWARD'S

NOTED SPECTACLES

FROM 1/- PER PAIR. THE EYES TESTED.

157, KIRKDALE ROAD.

Above: Jim sold programmes for the Theatre Royal in Breck Road while he was still at school

Cotton Exchange in Old Hall Street, 1928. Jim worked for A Hannay and Co Cotton Merchants from when he left school, aged 14, in 1916. In its heyday, this was the commercial centre of the North West, with the main trader being the USA

Left: Vine Street, 1968. On the right is St Catherine's Hall where 'Jim Mac's band' made their debut

Below: Walton Hall Avenue, 1938. The 44 tram is heading to the Pier Head. This is the route Jim would take to work from Norris Green

Aged 14 Jim left school and started working for A Hannay and Co Cotton Merchants. It was 1916 and war was raging in Europe.

After the war, Jim formed his own band, the 'Masked Melody Makers'. The name was then changed to 'Jim Mac's band'. Jim used his contacts from his younger theatre days to get bookings in dance halls around Liverpool. They made their debut at St Catherine's Hall, on Vine Street.

Jim reached the title of cotton salesman, which was unusual for a working-class man, and the band were getting bookings. However, in 1927 his dad Joe died, aged 60. Shortly after his death, Florrie moved the family to a new home at ***11 Scargreen Avenue, Norris Green***, off the East Lancashire Road.

Life was different in Scargreen Avenue. It was a new house with all mod cons, gas, electricity and front and back gardens. Jim appointed himself head gardener, having developed green fingers tending the gardens of Mr Hannay, from the cotton company who employed him, in Heswall.

Norris Green was a new estate on the outskirts of the city. It would take Jim a 20 to 30-minute tram ride along the East Lancashire Road, Walton Hall Avenue, Walton Lane, Scotland Road and Byrom Street to get to work.

St Charles Borromeo RC Church on Aigburth Road. Owen and Mary married here in 1905

CHAPTER 2
MOTHER MARY

OWEN MOHIN AND MARY THERESA DANHER (MATERNAL GRANDPARENTS)

Owen was born in Tullynamalrow, County Monaghan, Ireland, in 1880. Mary was born in Aigburth, Liverpool, in 1879. They ***married at St Charles Borromeo Roman Catholic Church***, Aigburth Road, on April 24 1905.

On the marriage lines Owen listed his address as 9 MacIntyre Street, Glasgow.

After the marriage, they moved from Aigburth Road to Third Avenue, Fazakerley. Owen was a gambler and now lived five minutes from Aintree racecourse.

They were both practising catholics. Mary stayed at home while Owen was busy making a living 'on the coal' as a coal merchant. The majority of homes in Liverpool were heated by coal.

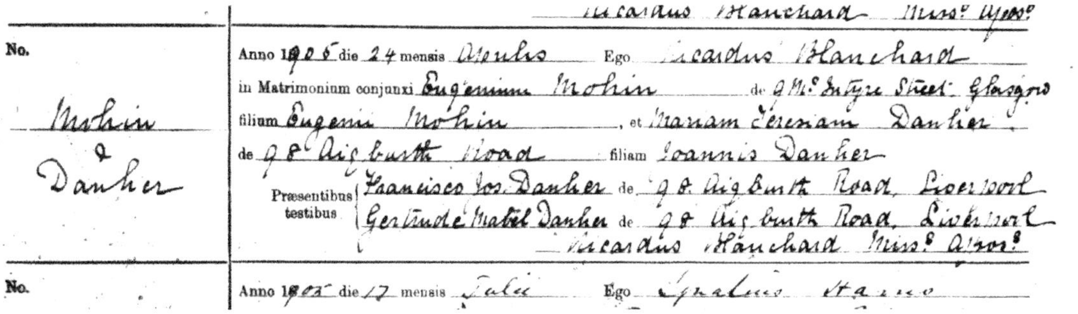
Ricardus Blanchard Miss. Ap.

No. Mohin & Danher

Anno 1905 die 24 mensis Aprilis Ego Ricardus Blanchard
in Matrimonium conjunxi Eugenium Mohin de 9 McIntyre Street Glasgow
filium Eugenii Mohin, et Mariam Teresiam Danher
de 98 Aigburth Road filiam Joannis Danher
Præsentibus testibus Francisco Jos. Danher de 98 Aigburth Road Liverpool
Gertrude Mabel Danher de 98 Aigburth Road Liverpool
Ricardus Blanchard Miss. Ap.

No. Anno 1905 die 17 mensis Julii Ego Ignatius Hanno

Marriage lines of Paul's maternal grandparents, Owen Mohin and Mary Danher

Right: Street directory for Third Avenue, Fazakerley. Owen is listed as living at number 2

Below: A horse-drawn coal wagon delivers essential supplies on Falkner Street, Liverpool, in 1934. This was Owen's job

THIRD AVENUE, FAZAKERLEY.
Longmoor lane Fazakerley
1 Wright John
3 Milner Thomas freight clerk
5 Williamson William J. warehousemn
7 Hunter Thomas
9 Brown Harry clerk
11 Holt Mrs. Elizabeth
13 Helsby George A. clerk
15 Dobbins John
19 Meakin Herbert blacksmith
21 Haigh Edward James iron driller
23 Cowpland James pottery turner
25 Silcock Mark
27 Whalley Miss Annie
33 Nicolls Arthur bricklayer
35 Griffin John labourer
37 Humphreys Mrs. Mary
41 Crook Charles
2 Mohin Owen coal merchant
4 Whitfield Thomas wheelwright
6 Charnock John butcher
8 Hyland Mrs. Elizabeth
10 Bermingham John machinist
12 Arthur Miss Mary E.
14 Charnock Roger R. signalman
18 Kirk Hugh goods checker
20 Sutherland Mrs. Grace
22 Peterson Victor ship's carpenter
24 Draffin John
28 Lockley Mrs. Ann
32 Forshaw Mrs. Alice
34 Cannell John James compositor
38 Anderton James railway clerk
40 Amson John joiner
42 Smith Sidney H.
44 Williams Mrs. Ada E.
46 McMurray James joiner

Third Avenue, Fazakerley, as it looks today. The house at the end of the terrace is number 2

THIRD
AVENUE L9
DE03 UYL

MARY MOHIN

Paul McCartney's mother, ***Mary, was born on September 29 1909*** at 2 Third Avenue.

Shortly after Mary's birth she was taken to the Blessed Sacrament RC Church, Walton Vale, to be baptised. The date was October 17 1909.

Mary senior decided to move the family to a new house at 19 Warbreck Moor, Walton. The benefit of the new home was that it had a shop. The money Owen had made on the coal meant he could afford to retire and run the shop with her.

MARY LOSES HER MUM AND SISTER

Mary's school was the Blessed Sacrament RC on Cedar Road, which was in the shadow of Hartley's jam factory on Long Lane. Her school was only a short walk from home, which she shared with her two brothers and younger sister.

When she was eight, in 1918, her baby sister, ***Agnes, died, aged two***, at Mill Road Hospital. Mary senior was grief-stricken and desperately wanted another child. Owen was worried because of her age (approaching 40) and the depression into which she had sunk. He thought another pregnancy could have devastating consequences. Mary was determined and found herself expecting another child within weeks.

In January 1919 Owen's fears were realised. His wife gave birth to a stillborn child and owing to complications was left severely weakened herself. ***Mary senior didn't recover and died a few days later.*** Mary junior, by then aged nine, had lost her mother and two siblings within a year.

Below: Mary's birth certificate, 1909. Below, right: Blessed Sacrament RC school, as it looks today

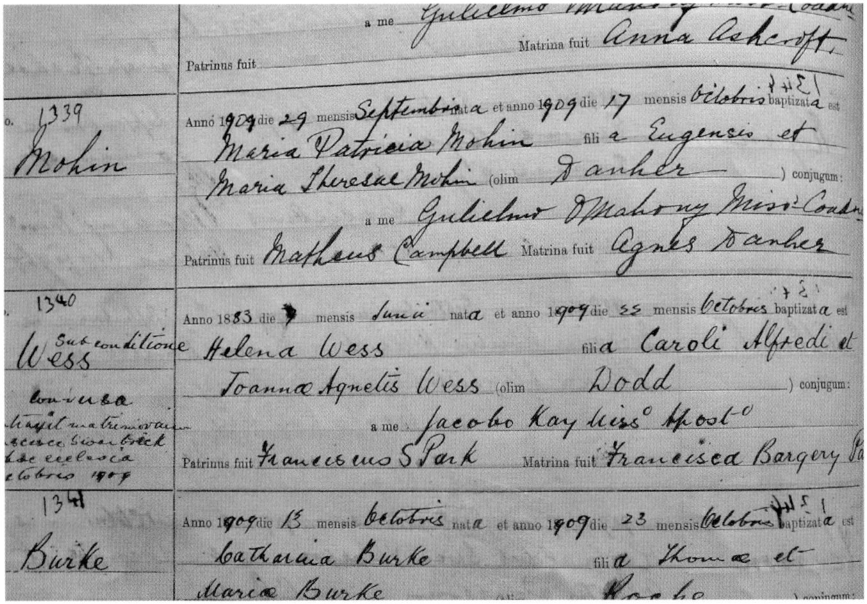

a me Gulielmo [illegible]
Patrinus fuit Matrina fuit Anna Ashcroft.

1339 Mohin
Anno 1909 die 29 mensis Septembris nata et anno 1909 die 17 mensis Octobris baptizata est
Maria Patricia Mohin filia Eugensio et
Maria Theresa Mohin (olim Danher) conjugum:
a me Gulielmo O'Mahony Miss. Coad.
Patrinus fuit Matheus Campbell Matrina fuit Agnes Danher

1340 Wess Sub conditione
Anno 1883 die [illegible] mensis Junii nata et anno 1909 die 25 mensis Octobris baptizata est
Helena Wess filia Caroli Alfredi et
Joanna Agnetis Wess (olim Dodd) conjugum:
a me Jacobo Kay Miss. Apost.
Patrinus fuit Franciscus Park Matrina fuit Francisca Bargery

1341 Burke
Anno 1909 die 13 mensis Octobris nata et anno 1909 die 23 mensis Octobris baptizata est
Catharina Burke filia Thomae et
Maria Burke

Blessed Sacrament RC Church, Walton Vale

Black Bull, Walton Vale, 1926. Paul's maternal grandparents and mum knew this area very well when they were living on Third Avenue and Warbreck Moor

Warbreck Moor, 1935, and Warbreck Moor shops as they looked in late 2009. The estate agents is based at number 19

Long Lane, Aintree, 1928. Hartley's jam factory is on the right. Mary's school, Blessed Sacrament RC, was very close to the factory on Cedar Road

Alder Hey Hospital, 1935. This is where Mary's nursing career began

Owen couldn't cope with the loss of his wife. In his grief he made a decision that was another devastating blow to Mary and her two brothers. He decided to move the family to his home country, Ireland. When they arrived, Owen tried his hand at farming. With him and his sons working in the fields, Mary found herself taking on the household chores: the washing, cooking, cleaning. She was only 11 years old.

After a few months in Ireland the farming idea collapsed, and Owen's gambling worsened, so with great relief to Mary, it was back to Liverpool to her friends.

MARY BECOMES A NURSE/MIDWIFE

When they arrived back in Liverpool, Owen returned to the coal business. In 1921, on a trip to Ireland to buy horses for his coal carts, he was introduced to a lady called Rose after a short business transaction involving £100. Owen was to marry Rose but this was not with the blessing of Mary.

Mary couldn't accept Rose as a stepmother or a replacement for her own mother. At the age of 13 she left home and went to live with her late mum's family, the Danhers.

Still haunted by the death of her mum, Mary decided to become a midwife, so that, if possible, she could prevent any other pregnant women dying in the way her own mother had.

At the age of 14, in 1923, Mary started a long nursing career at Alder Hey Hospital. She studied hard to gain the qualification she needed to fulfil the mission she had set herself.

After 10 years in the nursing profession, Mary, aged 24, qualified as a midwife and became a sister in the maternity ward of Walton Hospital. Now she was in a position to help the people she entered nursing to care for: expectant mothers.

It was about this time that Mary's father died. Owen and Rose were living at 181 Earl Road, Liverpool, but his death was registered in Ireland on August 19 1933 at Blackrock, Dundalk, County Louth (Rose died 15 years later, aged 61).

Walton Hospital, 1963. The iconic clock tower on a winter's day

[T]ODAY:
Mervyn Russell's
Film Fan Fare
SEE PAGE 4

SUNDAY EDT.
Evening Express
No. 21,220. LIVERPOOL, SATURDAY, SEPTEMBER 2, 1939. 1d.

TODAY:
"That's Their Stor[y]
By SEARCHLIGHT
SEE PAGE 4

BRITAIN AT WAR

ANNOUNCEMENT BY PREMIER AT 11-15 a.m.

"FIGHTING BRUTE FORCE, BAD FAITH, AND OPPRESSION"

GERMANY FAILS TO GIVE UNDERTAKING

[B]RITAIN, FRANCE AND POLAND STAND TOGETHER

[T]HE PREMIER BROADCAST AT 11.15 A.M. "WE ARE AT WAR WITH GERMANY."

[T]HE PREMIER SAID THAT NO UNDERTAKING HAD BEEN RECEIVED FROM GERMANY. "CONSEQUENTLY, THIS COUNTRY IS AT WAR WITH GERMANY."

You can imagine what a bitter blow it is to me that all my long struggle to win peace has failed.

Yet I cannot believe that there is anything more or anything different that I could have done that would have been more successful.

[H]ITLER WOULD NOT HAVE PEACE

Up to the very last, it would have been quite possible to arrange a peaceful and honourable settlement between Germany and Poland. But Hitler would not have it.

His action shows convincingly that there is no chance of expecting that this man will ever give up his intention of using force to gain his will and he can only be stopped by force.

This morning the British Ambassador in Berlin handed to the German Government a final Note stating that unless we heard from them by 11 o'clock that they were prepared at once to withdraw their troops from Poland a state of war would exist between us.

I have to tell you now that no such undertaking has been received and in consequence this country is at war with Germany.

We and France are today, in fulfilment of our obligations, going to the aid of Poland, so bravely resisting this wicked and unprovoked attack in her people," the Premier said.

[M]r. Chamberlain added: "Now may God bless you all. May we defend the right. It is evil things that we shall be fighting against—brute force, bad faith, injustice oppression and persecution, and against them I am certain that the right will prevail."

I AM speaking to you from the Cabinet room at 10, Downing-street. This morning the [Br]itish Ambassador in Berlin [ha]nded the German Government [an] official Note stating that unless [we hear]d from them by 11 o'clock ...

... were announced in a German broadcast on Thursday night Hitler did not wait to hear comments on them but ordered his troops to cross the Polish frontier.

"His action shows convincingly that there is no chance of expecting that this man will ever give up his practice of ...

... and now we have resolved to finish it, I know you will all play your part with calmness and courage."

ASSURANCES FROM EMPIRE.

At such a moment as this the assurances of support that we have received from the Empire are a source of profound encouragement to us.

CONTINUED FROM PRECEDING COLUMN

MR. GREENWOOD'S PLEDGE FOR LABOUR

Mr. A. Greenwood said: "The intolerable agony of suspense from which all of us have suffered is over. We now know the worst. The hated word war has been spoken by Britain in fulfilment of her pledged word. We have heard the war begin within the precincts of this House."

For 54 hours, Mr. Greenwood continued, Poland has stood alone at the portals of civilisation, defending us and all free nations and all that we stand for all that we hold dear. She stood with unexampled bravery and with epic heroism.

"Poland we greet as a comrade. To her we say 'Our hearts are with you, and with our hearts, all our power until the Angel of Peace returns to our midst,'" added Mr. Greenwood.

"In this titanic struggle, unparalleled, I believe, in the history of the world, Nazism must be finally overthrown.

"The Premier has given us his word that it shall be so, and so long as the relentless purpose is pursued with vigour, with foresight and with determination by the Government, so long there will be a united nation.

"But should there be confused counsels, inefficiency and wavering, then other men must be called to take their share.

"The Labour Party share no responsibility in the tremendous tasks which confront the Government, but had responsibilities of their own which they would not shirk.

Mr. Greenwood pledged the Labour Party that they would continue to give their full contribution to the National cause.

"May the war be swift and short, and the peace which follows stand proudly for ever on the shattered ruins of an evil name," added Mr. Greenwood.

Sir Archibald Sinclair, leader of the Liberal Opposition, after expressing sympathy with the Premier said: "It is the determination of Parliament to see this thing through."

"Let the world know that the British people are irrevocably determined to end this Nazi domination for ever, and build an order of peace and justice and freedom."

Mr. Winston Churchill said it was well to dwell for a moment on our repeated efforts for peace.

"Outside, the storms of war may blow and the lands may be lashed with the furies of its gales, but in our own hearts this Sunday morning there is peace," he added.

"Our hands may be active, but our consciences are at rest. We must not underrate the gravity of the task which lies before us, the severity of the ordeal.

"We must expect many disappointments and many unpleasant surprises, but we may be sure that the task which we have freely accepted is one not beyond the compass of the strength of the British Empire and the French Republic.

"The Premier said it was a sad day and that is indeed true," Mr. Churchill went on, "but it seems to me that there is another note which may be present at this moment, and that is a feeling of thankfulness that if these great trials were to come upon our island there is a generation of Britons here now ready to prove itself not unworthy of the days of yore and not unworthy of those great men, the fathers of our land, who have laid the foundations of our laws and shaped the greatness of our country."

"PESTILENCE OF NAZI TYRANNY"

"This is no question of fighting for Danzig or fighting for Poland. We are fighting to save the whole world from the pestilence of Nazi tyranny and in defence of all that is most sacred to man.

"This is no war domination, for imperial aggrandisement, for material ...

LATEST

FRENCH ULTIMATUM TO GERMANY.

French Ambassador informed German Government that Germany, aggressive act, threatening Poland's independence created conditions which called for carrying out British and French guarantees to Poland.

Failing satisfactory assurance that German Government had totally suspended all aggressive action against Poland, and was ready promptly to withdraw forces, French Government would without hesitation fulfil obligation in regard to Poland.—Ex. Tel.

TRAMCAR SERVICES CURTAILED.

Commencing today, Sunday 3rd, September, the frequency of all Tramway Services will be reduced after Sunset and from 10.30 p.m. Skeleton services only will be operated and only on the main routes at intervals of 15 or 30 minutes until the time of the last normal car.

GERMANY'S REPLY POINTS.

Germany's note rejecting the ultimatum asserts German pepole were not in a position to accept or fulfil any British ultimatum, alleges that British Government nullified all German attempts at a peaceful settlement; contends that the British Government approved and encouraged the Polish steps against Danzig and the German minority. German Government could not tolerate conditions on its Eastern border "similar to those in Palestine. German Government, therefore, rejects ultimatum to withdraw German troops.—B.U.P.

Cinema And Theatre Ban

Government have given instructions for all cinemas, theatres, and other places of entertainment to be closed immediately until further notice. Sports gatherings, indoor or outdoor, which involve large numbers congregating, are prohibited until further notice. Churches and other places of worship will not be closed.

All day schools in evacuation and neutral areas in England, Wales and Scotland are to be closed for lessons for at least a week from today

In reception areas, schools will be opened as soon as evacuation is complete.

The following advice is given:

Keep off the streets as much as possible; to expose yourself unnecessarily adds to your danger.

Make sure all members of your household have on them their names and addresses clearly written.

Do this on an envelope or luggage label, and not on an odd piece of paper which may be lost.

Sew a label on children's clothing so that they cannot pull it off.

CALL TO DOCTORS

Doctors under Ministry of Health Emergency Medical service who were asked to report automatically for whole time duty at specified hospitals, should now report accordingly.

HEAVY FIGHTING IN "CORRIDOR"

GERMANS BOMB HOSPITAL

POLES CLAIM 37 ENEMY 'PLANES DOWN

WARSAW, Saturday night.

CASUALTIES on both sides are reported to be heavy in the fighting in Pomorze, the "Corridor" province of Poland, where the German pressure is stated to be increasing. An official spokesman in Warsaw said the Germans on Friday occupied Zbaszyn and Myszniec along the southern section of Poland's East Prussian border because the Poles were by then not up to the border line.

Paris reports say that the Warsaw wireless has been heard announcing that the 16th century cloisters and other buildings in the Polish holy city of Czestochowa, near the frontier north of Cracow, are on fire. Reports reaching Paris from Brussels say that Germany is understood to be preparing for the biggest engagement yet.

HOSPITAL RAID

CALLING IN AGE GROUPS

MR. HORE-BE[LISHA] TELLS OF GO[VERNMENT] INTENTIO[N]

LABOUR AMENDMENT BILL

THE age limit ... National Servi[ce] Forces) Bill was discu[ssed in the] House of Commons, tod[ay].

Mr. Hore-Belisha, replyin[g to an] amendment to increase the ... from 18 to 20, assured the ... this lower age group would ... last classes to be called u[p].

He shared the view that ... undesirable to place the pr... of war on those in the lowe[r] ... but it so happened that i[n the] ... Army the age was 18, and ... Army it was 17.

"I think, therefore, no ... would be served in carryi[ng] ... ment of this kind when ... defending Poland," said ... Belisha.

OUR PRESENT POS[ITION]

We now had all the men ... he added, except certai[n] ... tradesmen.

There were 240,000 men ... June last, on whose ser[vices] ... not yet completely calle[d] ... would be many of the ... group now under obliga[tion] ... who would have to be tra[ined].

It would therefore be so[me time before] we called upon any other ...

"In the next age group, ... from the point from which ... started," Mr. Hore Belisha ... is our intention at the ... shall go up the scale ver[y] ... before we contemplate pla[cing any obli]gation upon men of 18.

"Let us hope," Mr. ... added, "that we shall ge[t through the] whole of this war without ... upon them at all."

Mr. Hore-Belisha, repl[ying to Mr.] Alexander, said: "At this ... we are taking out of the ... prepared for overseas all ... in the Army who are und[er] ... are not intending to se[nd] ... France although they hav[e] ... regular soldiers.

"It will show the Ho[use] ... tude with which we appro[ach] ...

NEW FRE[NCH] DEMARCHE IN ...

M. Coulondre, French ... Berlin, will call on Herr ... at noon today, to obtain ... last French communi[cation] ... Germany's aggression ag[ainst] ...

He will transmit a ... from the French Gover[nment to the] Reich.

NOT AN ENEMY

The Air Ministry a... eleven thirty a.m. an ... observed approaching th... As its identity could ... determined an air raid ... given. It was short[ly] ... identified as a friendly ...

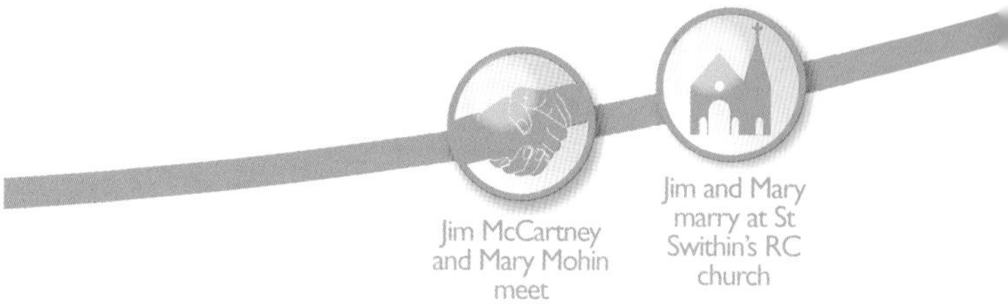

CHAPTER 3
GOT TO GET YOU INTO MY LIFE

Front page of the Evening Express newspaper, announcing the outbreak of war

THE SECOND WORLD WAR

Jim was happy, settling down as a contented bachelor with the role of head of the house in Scargreen Avenue. Then war broke out.

Between 1939 and 1940, a large number of false air-raid warnings sounded and mothers started to bring their children, who had been evacuated to safe areas, back home. The civilian defence committee knew that the city could come under attack at any time and discouraged families from returning to Liverpool.

In August 1940, the phoney war ended. On the 17th, the air-raid alert sounded. Because there had been so many false alarms, people were in no rush to get to the shelters, until explosions could be heard in the docks. The sound carried all around the city, the Luftwaffe had arrived and the war had come to Liverpool.

Between 1940 and 1942 the area was bombed repeatedly. The heaviest and most sustained attack came in May 1941 when wave after wave of German bombers flew over the city.

Jim wasn't able to enlist because of his age (37 in September 1939) and the childhood accident that left him with impaired hearing. That didn't stop him from doing his bit. He worked at Napier's Aircraft Factory, on the East Lancashire Road, and in the evenings he was a firewatcher in the city centre.

The role of a firewatcher was to stay in a building during an air raid. The protection they had was a whistle, a hard hat, a bucket of sand and a stirrup pump. If an incendiary bomb landed on their building they had to extinguish it before a fire took hold. The Germans dropped incendiary bombs so that their heavy bombers could use the fires as targets.

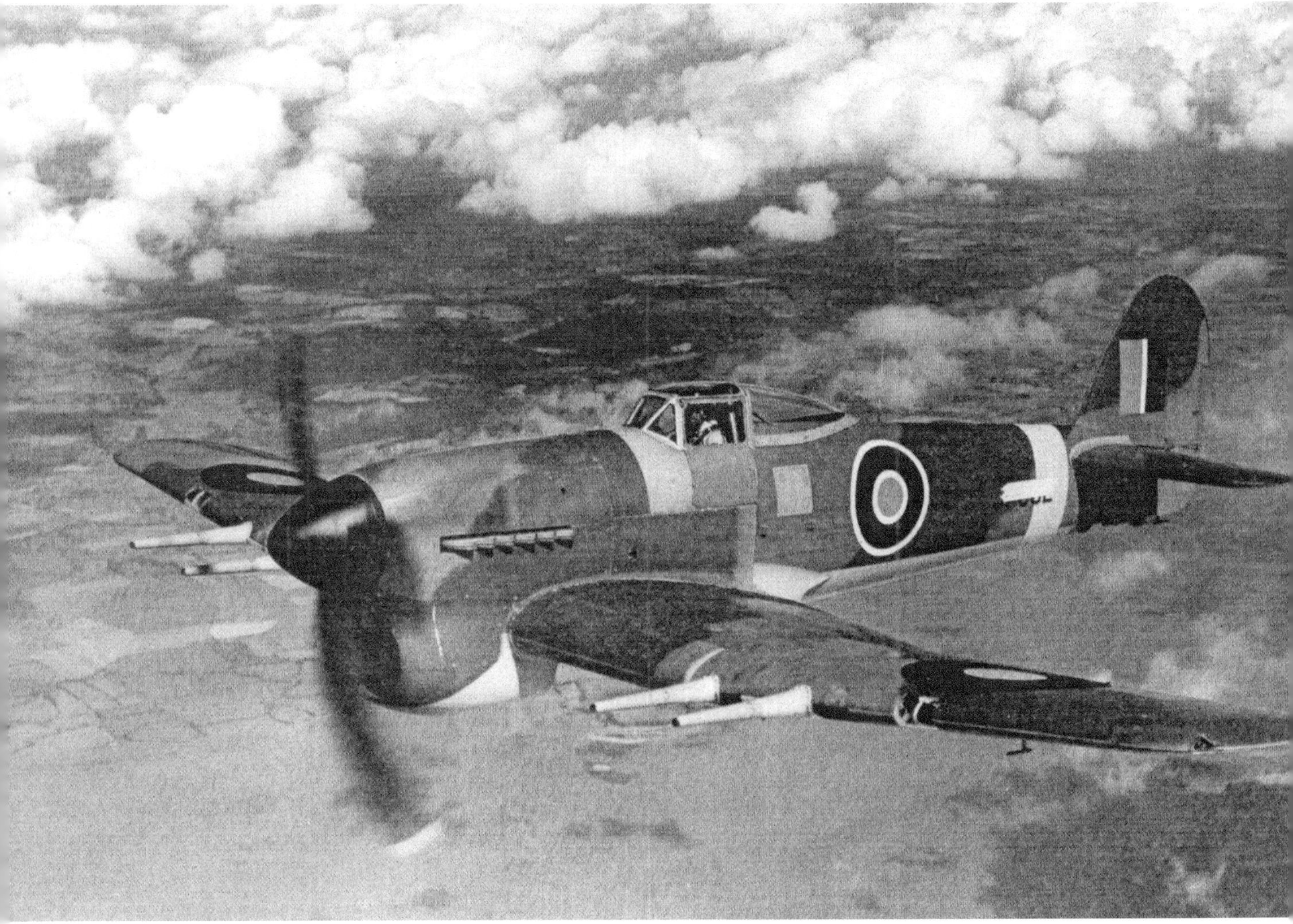

A Typhoon aeroplane. The engines for this aircraft were built at Napier's

Fieldton Road, 1956. This is where Mary was lodging when she met Jim

Fieldton Road as it is today

Scargreen Avenue. Number 11 is the one with a tree in the front

After every raid families would run around to each other's homes to reassure their loved ones that all was well. It was after one of the early raids that Jim's newly-married sister, Jin, and her friend, who was staying with her at the time, went to visit Jin's mother (Florrie) in Scargreen Avenue.

While they were there, the air-raid siren sounded, which meant they had to stay there until the all-clear had sounded. Jim was also at home that evening and the friend Jin had brought with her was a nursing sister from Walton Hospital, Mary Mohin.

JIM AND MARY

From the night Jim and Mary met, they were inseparable. These two people from completely different backgrounds just clicked and were head over heels in love. After a short romance in war-torn Liverpool, they started to plan their wedding. Jim was still living at Scargreen Avenue, while Mary was lodging less than a mile away at Fieldton Road. Mary's parish was ***St Swithin's, Gillmoss, and they married at that church on April 15 1941.***

St Swithin's Church in Gillmoss, 1939. Jim and Mary married here two years after this picture was taken

The marriage lines of Jim and Mary

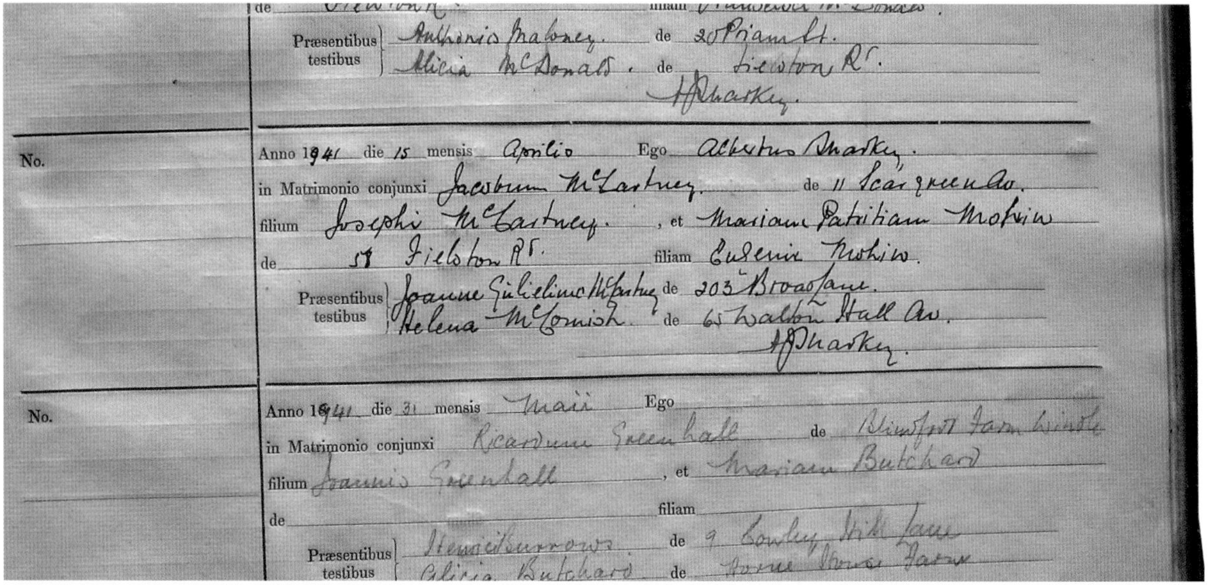

Præsentibus testibus Antonio Maloney de 20 Priam St.
Alicia McDonald de Fieldton Rd.
A. Sharkey.

No.
Anno 1941 die 15 mensis Aprilis Ego Albertus Sharkey
in Matrimonio conjunxi Jacobum McCartney de 11 Scargreen Av.
filium Josephi McCartney, et Mariam Patritiam Mohin
de 57 Fieldton Rd. filiam Eugenii Mohin.
Præsentibus testibus Joannes Gulielmus McCartney de 203 Broad Lane.
Helena McGonnish de 65 Walton Hall Av.
A. Sharkey.

No.
Anno 1941 die 31 mensis Maii Ego
in Matrimonio conjunxi Ricardum Greenhall de
filium Joannis Greenhall, et Mariam Butchard
de filiam
Præsentibus testibus de 9 Lane
Alicia Butchard de Farm

The site of St Swithin's Church, as it looks today. This building is now a community centre offering vocational training

Left and right: 10 Sunbury Road, where Jim and Mary shared their first home

On the night Jim and Mary married, the celebrations were cut short because air-raid sirens sounded, just like on the evening they met. They had to spend the first evening as husband and wife in the shelter with the rest of the family.

Because of the shortage of houses in Liverpool, it was customary for newly-married couples to live with one of their parents. That idea didn't suit Mary, so they would both regularly check the adverts in the Liverpool Echo newspaper for a place of their own. It wasn't long before they found something and moved to their first home together, which was to be furnished rooms at 10 Sunbury Road, Anfield.

Mary carried on working at Walton Hospital, and because of the large number of air-raid casualties she was working double shifts. Jim was still at Napier's and in the evenings he was firewatching. Mary knew of the dangers and every time Jim walked out of the door wearing his hard hat, it might have been the last time she'd see him alive. Being a religious woman she'd pray to all her saints to bring him home safely, which they always did.

92

CHAPTER 4
GOOD DAY SUNSHINE

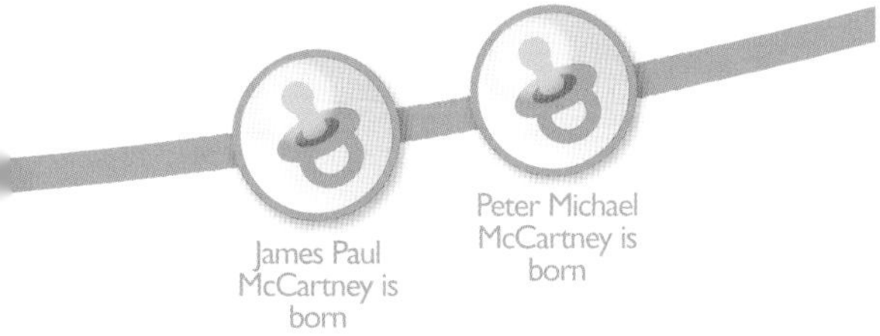

Opposite: 92 Broadway Avenue, as it's now known

PAUL'S BIRTH

Within a few months of being married, Mary became pregnant. Jim was overjoyed with the news; he couldn't believe he was going to be a dad.

On June 18 1942, in a private ward in Walton Hospital, little James Paul McCartney was born. Big Jim was delighted; he was cut out for fatherhood. When they returned home to Sunbury Road, the proud parents decided to call their first child by his second name, Paul. He was baptised as a catholic at St Philomena's church, across the road from Scargreen Avenue, on July 12, as the Orange Lodge were holding their annual parade.

By June 1942, the raids on Liverpool had stopped, but Jim was still working at Napier's. Being classified as Air Force he was offered a house in Wirral. After discussing it with Mary, the three of them moved to 92 Broadway, Wallasey.

Within a few months of moving across the Mersey, Jim's job at Napier's had finished. This meant the rent in Wallasey was unaffordable so they were forced to move into a pre-fab bungalow in Roach Avenue, Knowsley. Pre-fabs were used as short-term accommodation while the city was re-built.

It was a hard time for Jim and Mary, but it wasn't long before he found himself a job as an inspector for Liverpool Corporation cleansing department. Mary had taken time out of nursing to look after baby Paul, so money was a bit tight.

A SECOND CHILD

Mary was to make another announcement to Jim; she was pregnant again. If Jim was pleased the first time round, this time he was overcome with happiness. It was back to Walton Hospital and on January 7 1944 a belated Christmas present arrived for Paul, a baby brother called Peter Michael McCartney. Once again, when Mary and Jim returned home to Roach Avenue, they decided to drop the first name and call him by his second name, Michael.

Paul's baptism lines

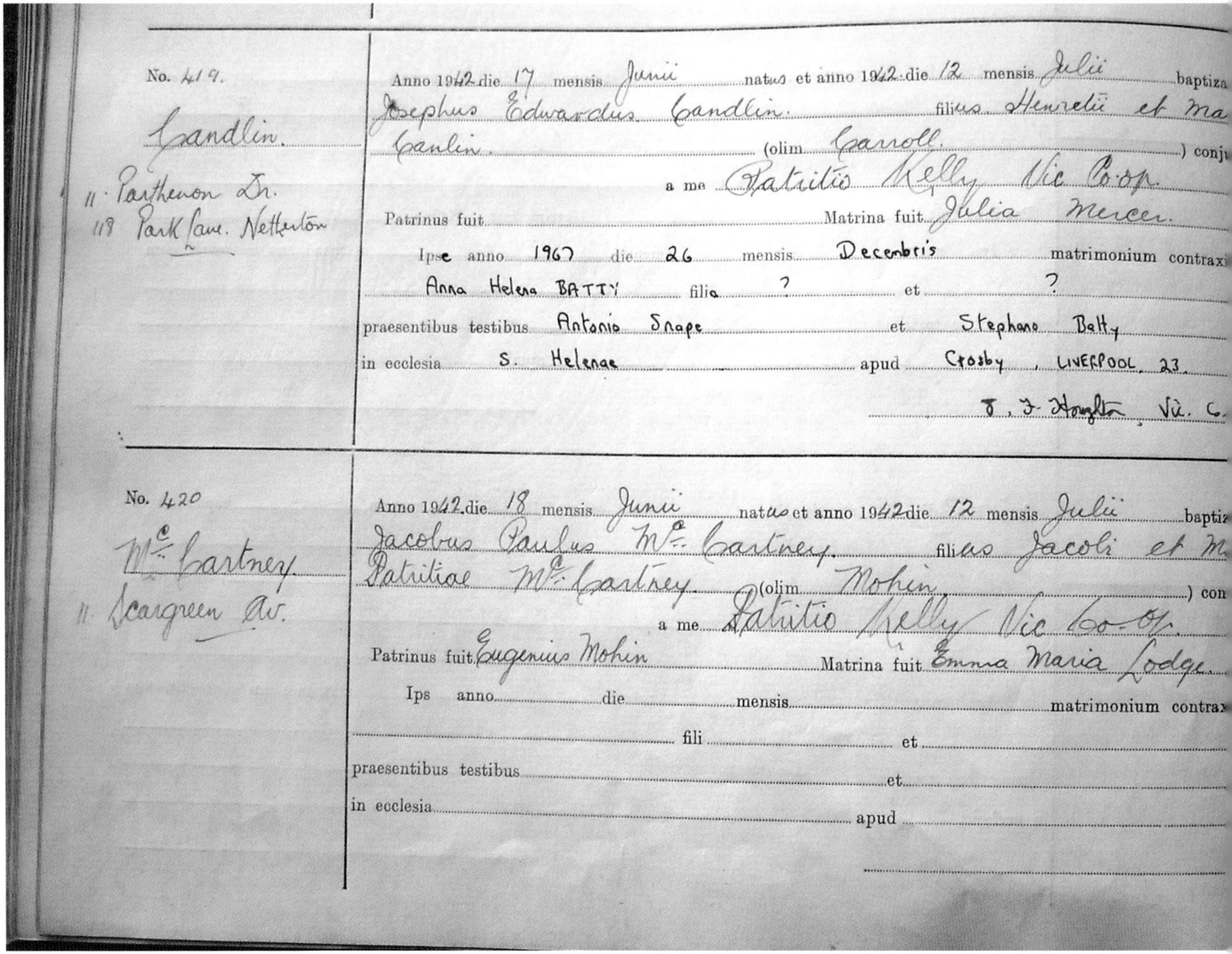

No. 419.

Candlin.

11 · Parthenon Dr.

118 Park Lane. Netherton

Anno 1942 die 17 mensis Junii natus et anno 1942 die 12 mensis Julii baptiza

Josephus Edwardus Candlin. filius Henrici et ma

Canlin. (olim Carroll.) conju

a me Patritio Kelly Vic Co-op.

Patrinus fuit Matrina fuit Julia Mercer.

Ipse anno 1967 die 26 mensis Decembris matrimonium contrax

Anna Helena BATTY filia ? et ?

praesentibus testibus Antonio Snape et Stephano Batty

in ecclesia S. Helenae apud Crosby, LIVERPOOL 23.

J. J. Houghton, Vic. C.

No. 420

McCartney

11 Scargreen Av.

Anno 1942 die 18 mensis Junii natus et anno 1942 die 12 mensis Julii baptiz

Jacobus Paulus McCartney. filius Jacobi et M

Patritiae McCartney (olim Mohin) con

a me Patritio Kelly Vic Co-Op.

Patrinus fuit Eugenius Mohin Matrina fuit Emma Maria Lodge

Ips anno die mensis matrimonium contrax

fili et

praesentibus testibus et

in ecclesia apud

Right: Typical pre-fab housing, 1950s

Below: East Lancs Road, 1957. Rows and rows of pre-fab housing. In the background on the left is Napier's factory

The old Walton Hospital as it looks today. This building has been converted into residential apartments. In late 2009 a smaller teaching hospital was still open, to the right of this structure

X-ray Department

LAST CITY
Evening Express
No. 21,960 LIVERPOOL, TUESDAY, MAY 8, 1945 THREE-HALFPENCE

Premier Broadcasts Details Of German Surrender, Reveals—

HOSTILITIES END 12.1 A.M.

Agreement Will Be Ratified in Berlin

RESISTANCE: A WARNING

[T]AKING his big broadcast to the nation and Empire this afternoon, Mr. Churchill said:—

[Y]esterday morning at 2.41 a.m. at General Eisenhower's Headquarters, General Jodl, [r]epresentative of the German High Command and of Grand-Admiral Doenitz, [d]esignated head of the German State, signed an act of unconditional surrender of all [G]erman land, sea and air forces in Europe to the Allied Expeditionary Forces, and [s]imultaneously to the Soviet High Command.

General Bedell Smith, Chief of Staff of the United States Army, and General [illegible], signed the document on behalf of the Supreme Commander of the Allied Expeditionary Force, and General [illegible] signed on behalf of the Russian High Command.

"Today this agreement will be ratified and confirmed at Berlin, where Air Chief Marshal Tedder, Deputy Supreme Commander of the Allied Expeditionary Force, and General Tassigny, will sign on behalf of General Eisenhower. General Zhukov will sign on behalf of the Soviet High Command.

The German representatives will be Field Marshal Keitel, Chief of the High Command, and Commanders-in-Chief of the German Army, Navy and Air Forces.

"Hostilities will end officially at one minute after midnight tonight, Tuesday, 8th May, one minute after midnight, but in the interests of saving lives the "cease fire" began yesterday, to be sounded all along the front, and our dear Channel Islands are also to be freed today.

Attack On Rebels From All Points

"The Germans are still in places resisting the Russian troops, but [illegible]

[illegible]

not for a moment the toil and efforts that lie ahead.

"Japan, with all her treachery and greed, remains unsubdued. The injury she has inflicted on Great Britain, the United States and other countries, and her detestable cruelties, call for justice and retribution.

"We must now devote all our strength and resources to the completion of our task both at home and abroad.

"Advance Britannia! Long live the cause of freedom. God save the King."

Mr. Churchill's message was followed immediately by the ceremonial sounding of the end of the war in Europe by the buglers of the [illegible] Guards.

Splash Of Colour

There was a splash of colour about the Commons VE-Day sitting. When the House met for prayers at 2.15, the Speaker (Colonel Clifton Brown), the Serjeant at Arms (Brigadier Sir Charles Howard), and the Chaplain (Canon Don), were wearing the full robes of their offices.

The Speaker was in his black robe [e]mbroidered with gold braid and with white lawn cuffs; the Serjeant at Arms in his ornate silver and black dress and wearing his campaign medals and decorations, and Canon Don in scarlet and purple.

But for this, however, the House [illegible]

"Foul Aggression"

[illegible]

In The Lords

There was an air of expectancy when the House of Lords met this afternoon. Besides a large attendance of Peers, there were a number of Peeresses and their children, and the [illegible]

[illegible]

SCENES [A]T TOWN HALL

[L]ord Mayor Of [Liv]erpool's Speech

[illegible]

[R]emember Japs

[illegible]

Liverpool R.N. VE-Service

AT today's Royal Navy VE-thanksgiving service at Liverpool Pier Head. Below: a group of Wrens who attended. Bottom: (from left) Capt. G. [illegible] Hewitt; the Rev. [illegible], senior naval chaplain; Rear-Admiral J. W. S. Dorling.

The Beaten Army Goes Home

A BEATEN and silent army is going home.

Thousands upon thousands of men of the German army in Denmark, some pushing carts and prams, others riding in ambulances and some on horseback, are streaming along the roads leading to the south.

They pass their victors, British troops, going north on their way to take over in Denmark, wires Ronald Clark, B.U.P.

The Germans are completely ignored by the population.

★

GERMANS tried one of their last double crosses in the great Czech arms city of Pilsen—and it failed.

Holding white flags, the Germans allowed an Allied tank column to pass a building without firing.

Then when the last tank had gone by they cut loose with everything they had. After a two-hour battle in the main square the town fell, says Robert Richards, B.U.P.

★

W[ES] Gallagher, Associated Press war correspondent, [illegible]

★

GERMAN General George Von [illegible] [illegible]

Liverpool Cheers the Finale

Cheers and waving of Union Jacks greeted the arrival of the Lord Mayor and Lady Mayoress (Lord and Lady Sefton) as they stepped to the front of the balcony.

In the Lord Mayor's party were Admiral Sir Max Horton, Brig. J. H. Hardy, M.C., Rear-Admiral J. W. S. Dorling, the Archbishop of Liverpool (Dr. R. Downey), the Dean of Liverpool (Dr. F. W. Dwelly), Sir Andrew McNair (Vice-Chancellor of Liverpool University), Mr. C. Porter Kuykendall (Consul-General for U.S.A.), Mr. A. E. Bryan (Canadian Trade Commissioner), Ald. A. E. Shennan and Ald. Luke Hogan.

The Lady Mayoress waved her hand to the crowd which, despite the rain, extended half-way down Castle-street.

Long before three o'clock, crowds gathered on St. George's Plateau. [A] hush fell over the crowd as the Premier began his historic speech.

There were deafening cheers when he proclaimed the war in Europe at an end.

At 3.2 p.m. the first hooter rang across the waters of the Mersey, followed by the [illegible] of one of the smaller ships. The ferry boats at the quayside began [illegible]

'NOT THE END'

Says Prince Olaf

Crown Prince Olaf, as Commander-in-Chief of the Norwegian Armed Forces, today [illegible]

[illegible]

HOW THE NATION IS CELEBRATING

Huge Crowds At The Palace

LONDON, symbolic centre of the world celebrations and thanksgiving for victory in Europe, was early astir again today, ready to celebrate the real VE-Day—after last night's unofficial "mafficking."

Buckingham Palace was [illegible] attraction No. 1. Groups of people arrived there before 8 a.m., and during the day the crowd gradually grew into a [illegible] army, [illegible] as they packed all the approaches and crowded like ants on the base of the Queen Victoria Memorial.

The personal standard of the King—which is much larger than the normal one flown when the King is in residence—was flying over the Palace.

The bells of St. Paul's Cathedral this morning [illegible] the City of London to [illegible] thanksgiving, and the cathedral was packed with hundreds of workers from city offices. The singing of the hymn "Now thank we all our God," could be clearly heard in the streets outside.

Celebrations are going on all over the country, with cities, towns, villages, hamlets and lonely outposts gay with their flags and bunting, their streamers, symbols and emblems.

Despite the rainy weather on Merseyside, Liverpool and its neighbouring towns set out to make it a real public holiday and a memorable celebration.

Many of the poorer quarters had striking displays of flags and decorations; and in some cases the whole sides of street are said to have been converted into carefully painted Union Jacks.

(Celebrations on Merseyside, Deeside and in other areas are reported on Page Three.)

Investiture

AT 11 a.m. the King held the first investiture of peace-time at Buckingham Palace.

By a coincidence, the VE-Day ceremony was a presentation of medals won by "other ranks"—at 11 o'clock on the morning of D-Day, last June, the King held a similar function at the Palace.

First man to be decorated after the end of the war was Major Lewis Tevendale, Leicestershire Regiment, of Stonehaven, who won the Distinguished Conduct Medal as a sergeant-major at the Litani River in Syria, in June, 1941.

Early today the King was busy sending telegrams of congratulation to the Heads of State of the United Nations.

There were early indications that Buckingham Palace would be the No. 1 centre of attraction. Before 8 a.m. groups of people arrived to gaze at the Royal residence.

Standing on the steps of the Queen Victoria Memorial was A.C. [illegible] Bithell, aged 25, of the R.I.P., who had come from the Cambridge district. [illegible] Fit.-Lieut. Bithell, aged 23, [illegible]

"My mother and father are coming from [illegible], North Wales. They [illegible]

First big thrill of the day for the big crowds outside Buckingham Palace came when an open car drove through the Palace gates, carrying the Prime Minister on his way to lunch with the King and Queen—his first meeting with his sovereign since the war ended.

Mr. Churchill smiled and gave the V sign time and time again to the cheering crowd.

Thousands of people also lined Whitehall, where Mr. Churchill was expected to appear on the balcony of Ministry of Health this afternoon.

Service men and women marched arm-in-arm through London, singing lustily, waving flags, ribbons and flowers.

Conductresses of many packed buses abandoned all hope of [collecting] fares.

The King and Queen appeared on the balcony of Buckingham Palace with the two Princesses at 11 minutes past three and waved to the cheering crowd for three minutes.

QUEEN MAY BROADCAST

The Queen is expected to broadcast to the women of the Empire in the near future. Her talk will be a companion piece to the tribute she paid to them just over two years ago.

Radio experts say the Queen is an ideal broadcaster, with a natural microphone technique. The first broadcast she made as Queen was in September, 1938, at the launching of the Queen Elizabeth.—London Star.

On Other Pages

Warning of Food Scarcity

WITH the world short of food, there could be no relaxation of the food production drive, said Mr. R. S. Hudson, Minister of Agriculture, at the annual luncheon of the Newspaper Society in London, today.

"We in this country will need a maintenance of maximum effort by our farmers and farm workers," he said. "They, in turn, will need maximum help from the civilian population, even after taking into account the maximum use of prisoners of German and Italian prisoners.

"One of the things which has always [illegible] the [illegible] about the food production campaign is the relatively short [illegible] to which we have been forced to [illegible]

[illegible]

Thanks

Mr. Hudson today sent messages to the agricultural community and to the fishing industries. To the agricultural community he stated:

[illegible]

COAST BLACK-OUT: 10.37 p.m. to 5.39 a.m.

STOP PRESS

PREMIER'S RECEPTION

[illegible]

NAZI SALUTE GOES

[illegible] Associated Press.

HITLER'S BODY FOUND?

Russian troops have found body [illegible] to be Hitler's in ruins of Berlin, says a Red Army [illegible]—Associated Press.

DR. C. RANKIN

Death Of Noted Liverpool [illegible]

IT WILL BE

CHAPTER 5
WE CAN WORK IT OUT

Opposite: The front page of the Evening Express announces the end of the war. While Britain rejoiced, Jim was mourning his mum

MARY GOES BACK TO WORK AND FLORRIE'S DEATH

While Mary was in hospital giving birth to Michael, she realised how much she missed nursing, having taken a break for two years to bring up and care for Paul. She decided that once the time was right she would return to the job she loved. When the war came to an end on May 8 1945, Paul was nearly three and Michael was 16 months old.

While the nation was celebrating the end of the war, Jim and Mary were in mourning, because the day before the German surrender, on May 7 1945, ***Jim's mum Florrie died aged 70***.

As most of Liverpool was marking VE day with street parties, Jim had his mother's funeral to arrange, and sad memories also came back to Mary of her own mother, who died in 1919, and her sister, Agnes.

Mary felt it was now time to go back into nursing. After the war, the health service was going through a major shake-up as the Labour government wanted to nationalise it. The new National Health Service was to be beneficial to Mary, for when she returned to nursing as a municipal midwife, she was able to work from home and was allocated a house which came with the job. The next McCartney home was on the ground floor of a block of tenements in Everton, at 75 Sir Thomas White Gardens.

When Jim moved back to Everton, the streets where he grew up, he realised how much it had changed and he wasn't happy living in the tenements.

Mary also couldn't settle. She was always setting goals for herself and her latest was to move from Sir Thomas White Gardens, which she thought wasn't the right environment in which to bring up her young boys. With Jim's support, she applied to the health committee for a transfer.

Above: Sir Thomas White Gardens, 1969. The McCartneys briefly lived in one of these tenements after the war

Right: List of voters in Sir Thomas White Gardens. Jim and Mary lived in number 75

BOROUGH OF LIVERPOOL—KIRKDALE DIV.—ST. DOMINGO WARD—No. 85. P

SIR THOMAS WHITE GARDENS, 5—*cont.*

2993	Jones, Mary E.	67c
2994	Jones, John Henry	67c
2995	Henshaw, Thomas	67d
2996	Henshaw, Edna M.	67d
2997	Birchall, Margaret	69
2998	Collings, James	69a
2999	Collings, Annie	69a
3000	Taylor, Samuel J.	69b
3001	Taylor, Agnes M.	69b
3002	Kerr, William Henry	69c
3003	Kerr, Lily	69c
3004	Lewis, William James	69d
3005	Lewis, Nancy	69d
3006	Parkinson, Eleanor D.	71
3007	Parkinson, William	71
3008	Cookson, Elsie	71a
3009	Duncan, Hannah	71b
3010	Duncan, William	71b
3011	Smith, Thomas H.	71c
3012	Davies, Francis M.	71d
3013	Davies, Emma I.	71d
3014	Brooks, Francis	73
3015	Ellis, Annie	73
3016	Ellis, Richard	73
3017	Ellis, Richard, Senr.	73
3018	Williams, James Victor	73a
3019	Williams, Catherine	73a
3020	Carmichael, Margaret	73a
3021	Butler, Annie E.	73b
3022	Bilsborrow, Mary E.	73b
3023	Bilsborrow, Thomas	73b
3024	Bilsborrow, Thomas G.	73b
3025	Blower, Isabella	73b
3026	Scarisbrick, James	73c
3027	Scarisbrick, Catherine	73c
3028	McCartney, James	75
3029	McCartney, Mary P.	75
3030	Crook, William	75a
3031	Crook, Kathleen	75a
3032	Macfie, Thomas L.	75b
3033	Macfie, Vera	75b
3034	Macfie, Christina	75b
3035	Simpson, William H.	75c
3036	Stratton, Ronald	75c
3037	Stratton, John	75c
3038	Stratton, Eleanor	75c
3039	Latham, Arthur H.	2
3040	Latham, Margaret M.	2
3041	Henderson, Lily G.	2a
3042	Henderson, John	2a
3043	Henderson, John William	2a
3044	Parry, Catherine	2b
3045	Parry, James	2b
3046	McCartney, Hugh	2c
3047	Owens, Elizabeth	2c
3048	Owens, Violet	2c
3049	Owens, George White	2c
3050	Crosbie, Walter	4
3051	Crosbie, George	4
3052	Crosbie, Elizabeth	4
3053	Crosbie, John	4
3054	Rowlands, Grace E.	4a
3055	Brislen, James	4b
3056	Brislen, Margaret	4b
3057	Williams, Emily	4b
3058	McDonough, Henry	6
3059	McDonough, Hannah	6
3060	McNee, Margaret	6a
3061	McNee, George	6a
3062	Simpson, Alice	6a
3063	Cairns, Albert E.	6b
3064	Cairns, Elizabeth	6b
3065	Butterfield, Edward	6c
3066	Butterfield, Elizabeth	6c
3067	O'Neill, Arthur D.	6d

SIR THOMAS WHITE GARDENS, 5—*cont.*

3068	Woods, Jane	6d
3069	O'Neil, Alice	6d
3070	McKinlay, Emily	8
3071	McKinlay, Hugh	8
3072	Lewis, Elizabeth	8a
3073	Lewis, James	8a
3074	Verdin, Arthur	8a
3075	Verdin, Lilian	8a
3076	Parkinson, Christine	8b
3077	Parkinson, Thomas	8b
3078	Clay, Richard T.	8c
3079	Clay, James	8c
3080	Clay, Joyce Mary	8c
3081	Clay, Annabell	8c
3082	Breden, Joseph	10
3083	Breden, Esther	10
3084	Williamson, Lilian	10a
3085	Hickman, Irene	10a
3086	Routledge, William J.	10b
3087	Routledge, Jessie	10b
3088	Roberts Muriel	10c
3089	Morris, Frances	10c
3090	Jones, Martha	10c
3091	Moore, Albert Edmund	10d
3092	Moore, Alice	10d
3093	Moore, John W.	10d
3094	Naylor, William G.	12
3095	Naylor, Phoebe	12
3096	Graham, Margaret	12a
3097	Graham, Ronald	12a
3098	Graham, Hugh Leo	12a
3099	Moorcroft, Ronald	12b
3100	Moorcroft, Ada L.	12b
3101	Stanton, Albert E.	12b
3102	Stanton, Margaret	12b
3103	Kirwan, Margaret J.	12c
3104	Woods, Agnes	12d
3105	Woods, Edward G.	12d
3106	Davies, Thomas	14
3107	Davies, Frances	14
3108	Liderth, Elsie M.	14a
3109	Liderth, John	14a
3110	Kirby, Charles	14b
3111	Kirby, Dora	14b
3112	Stinson, Catherine	14b
3113	Horrocks, George	14c
3114	Horrocks, Mary E.	14c
3115	Lewis, William	14d
3116	Lewis, Jane E.	14d
3117	Cleary, Irene	16
3118	McCall, Emily	16
3119	Rule, Lily	16
3120	O'Leary, Mary	16a
3121	O'Leary, Felix T. W.	16a
3122	Smith, William	16b
3123	Smith, Elizabeth	16b
3124	Smith, William, Junr.	16b
3125	Dalziel, Mithen James	16c
3126	Dalziel, Lilian	16c
3127	Fergus, Amy	16c
3128	Fergus, Robert	16c
3129	Higham, Henry	18
3130	Higham, Mary	18
3131	Wales, Mary	18
3132	Wales, Samuel	18
3133	Whiteside, Catherine	18a
3134	Whiteside, Peter	18a
3135	Williams, Harold	18b
3136	Williams, Eleanor H.	18b
3137	Higham, Sophia	18c
3138	Nicholls, Charles	18d
3139	Moffatt, Lilian	20
3140	Moffatt, Jas.	20
3141	Moffatt, Catherine	20
3142	Baxter, Wm.	20a

Right: The minutes of the health committee meeting from 1947 granting Mary her transfer from Sir Thomas White Gardens

Salary: £330 per annum, rising by annual increments of £15 to £435 per annum.

Mrs. Olive Clarke, S.C.M., aged 26 -
Salary: £310 per annum, rising by annual increments of £15 to £415, and one of £10 to £425 per annum.

(9) Municipal Midwife McCartney - Payment of Removal Expenses.

Read the following Report of the Medical Officer of Health, viz.:-

The Medical Officer reports that it has been found necessary to transfer Nurse McCartney from 75 Sir Thomas White Gardens to 72 Western Avenue, Speke. Nurse McCartney has incurred expense in removing her furniture to this address and as the transfer was effected in order to meet the convenience of the Midwifery Department, the Medical Officer recommends that she be paid a sum not exceeding £5 to cover her expenses, in accordance with the usual custom.

Resolved - That payment of removal expenses be authorised accordingly.

10) Additional Maternity and Child Welfare Clinic Sessions.

Read the following Report of the Medical Officer of Health, viz.:-

The Medical Officer of Health reports that in order to relieve overcrowding, additional weekly clinic sessions are re-

Below: Housewives do the shopping at the junction of Western Avenue and All Saints Road in Speke. The McCartneys moved to the area in 1947

Below: An aerial view of the Speke housing estate in 1952. The road leading to the roundabout from the bottom left of the picture is Western Avenue

Above: Western Avenue, 1944. The house in the foreground is number 82

Right: Speke continues to develop in the 1950s. Builders are hard at work

Luckily for Mary she didn't have to wait too long for her transfer from the tenements to be granted. In the summer of 1947, she was allocated a house on the outskirts of Liverpool in Speke, which was a new housing development. The latest McCartney address was to be a midwife's house at ***72 Western Avenue***.

By the time the family moved to Western Avenue, Jim had returned to his old job at Hannay's cotton merchants. The Speke estate was still getting built, but it was a step up from the tenements, and both of them were happy.

In the post-war baby boom Mary was kept very busy delivering the little cherubs of Speke, always on call, working nights and weekends. She was a loved and highly respected woman, and was a frequent sight on her midwife's bike going to her next delivery. These were the days when people had respect for the job she was doing and it was safe for her to ride her bike through the streets, day or night.

WESTERN AVENUE, Speke (19).

..Tarbock road.

LEFT SIDE.

15 Kay Jn. chargehand
17 Fawley Mrs. Edith
19 Nicholson Ernest
21 Lacey Edwin bricklyr
23 Crawford Rt. asst. works chemist
25 Mason Jas
27 Armstrong Chas. Edwd. driller
29 Butterfield Jsph. C. draughtsman
31 Curtis Chas. H. storekeeper
33 Orme Harold
35 Cottam Wm
37 Lunt Jn
39 Seddon Albt. Wm. grocer
41 Cummings Jn. A
43 Sinnott Edwd. Wm. inspector
45 Liggett Jn. R. engnr
47 Murdoch Wm. E. ship's cook
49 Moss Herbt
51 Furlong Thos
53 Beaumont Sidney
55 Adshead Geo. W. clerk
57 Neaien Jn
59 McDougall Mrs. Ethel
61 Waddington Wm. H. clerk
63 Smith Arth. butcher
65 Bird Eric machinist
67 Blake Harold storekeeper
69 Ralphs Ralph fitter

Stapleton av

71 Edwards Fred shuttle mkr
73 Cooper Jsph. David fitter
75 Fitzgerald Mrs. Bertha
77 Walsh Thos. fitter
79 Perkins Frank
81 Beechey Claude engnr
83 Davies Edwd. storekeeper
85 Rose Clifford
87 Roberts Thos. V
89 Bent Jsph. electrician
91 Thompson Wm
93 Langdale Oswald
95 Watson Wilfred
97 Thomas Jn
99 Reid Wm
101 Timms Fredk
103 Thomas Edwd
105 Kayes Harold
107 Hennessy Thos
109 Morley Fras. wood worker
111 Bolton Harold coppersmith
113 Quirk Wm. Jas. decrtr
115 Pound Howard J

46 Hughes Hy. storekeeper
48 Helm Thos. labourer
50 Ralph Frank
52 Gittins Geo. storekeeper
54 McAuley Hugh
56 Cunningham Rt. W
58 Woodroofe Rd. S. jeweller
60 Crawford Rt. labourer
62 Sawyer Wm. fitter
64 Wyness Edmnd. G. sheet metal wrkr
66 Rhodes Geo. Fredk. tool mkr
68 Coppock Rt. fitter

Blackrod av

70 Jones Rt. Maurice ship's steward
72 McCartney Mrs. Mary P. midwife
74 Cooper Herbt. Aug. fitter
76 Scarr H. M
78 Neilands Jas. L. fitter
80 Beattie Mrs. Elsie
82 Jeffery Harold T. fitter
84 Burgess Thos
86 Cahill Jsph. fitter
88 Starkey Edwd
90 Curtis Jsph
92 Hunter Mrs. Eliz
94 Rylands Jn. erector
96 George Wm. fitter
98 Meyer Mrs. Ellen
100 Hines Wltr
102 Ireland Bernard Fras
104 Gillman Abraham
106 Harvey David P. motor driver
108 Williams Gwynne
110 Doolan Jn
112 Matthews Fras
114 Dunn Hy
116 Quirk Wm. painter
118 Spreag Herbt. Wm
120 Leigh Thos. electrician
122 Barton Jn. bricksetter
124 Roberts Wm. clerk
126 Barnes Mrs. Eliz
126A Smith Stephen
128 Allen Thos. Arth
128A Hutchison Jsph

Tewit Hall rd

130 Pawlson Rt. labourer
130A Flood Jas. labourer
132 Hall Mrs. Lillian
132A Abbott Mrs. Gladys
134 Hayes Hy. fitter
136 Martin Thos. Hy. fitter
138 Lovatt Benj
140 Ryder Albt. Edwd
142 Mason Jas. Rd. foreman
144 Hatton Herbt
146 Harding Jn. joiner

Left: 1949 Western Avenue residents' list

Right: 72 Western Avenue today

CHAPTER 6 IT'S GETTING BETTER

THE BOYS START SCHOOL

When the time came for Paul and Michael to start school, Jim didn't want his boys to go to one of a Catholic denomination because he thought they spent too much time on religion and not enough on education. Mary agreed, and the boys' school was to be ***Stockton Wood Primary***, which was only a few streets away from their home.

MARY RESIGNS

In the late summer of 1950, Mary decided to give up her job as a midwife, to spend more time with Jim and her boys. This wasn't an easy decision to make and all through the summer of that year Mary and Jim discussed the implications.

They knew that the family would have to give up the house on Western Avenue, but the nights and weekend calls were taking a toll and she was missing her boys growing up. Jim knew that somehow they would get by and Mary's happiness was more important, so with that in mind she handed in her notice to the health committee in September 1950.

The McCartneys knew what was going to happen next. Sure enough, the letter from the health committee dropped through the door, telling Mary to vacate Western Avenue within one week of the date of the letter. She took the letter to the housing office and was quickly allocated another house; the next move for the family was to the back end of Speke, at 12 Ardwick Road.

Stockton Wood Primary School in 1973. This is how it would have looked when Paul and Michael went there

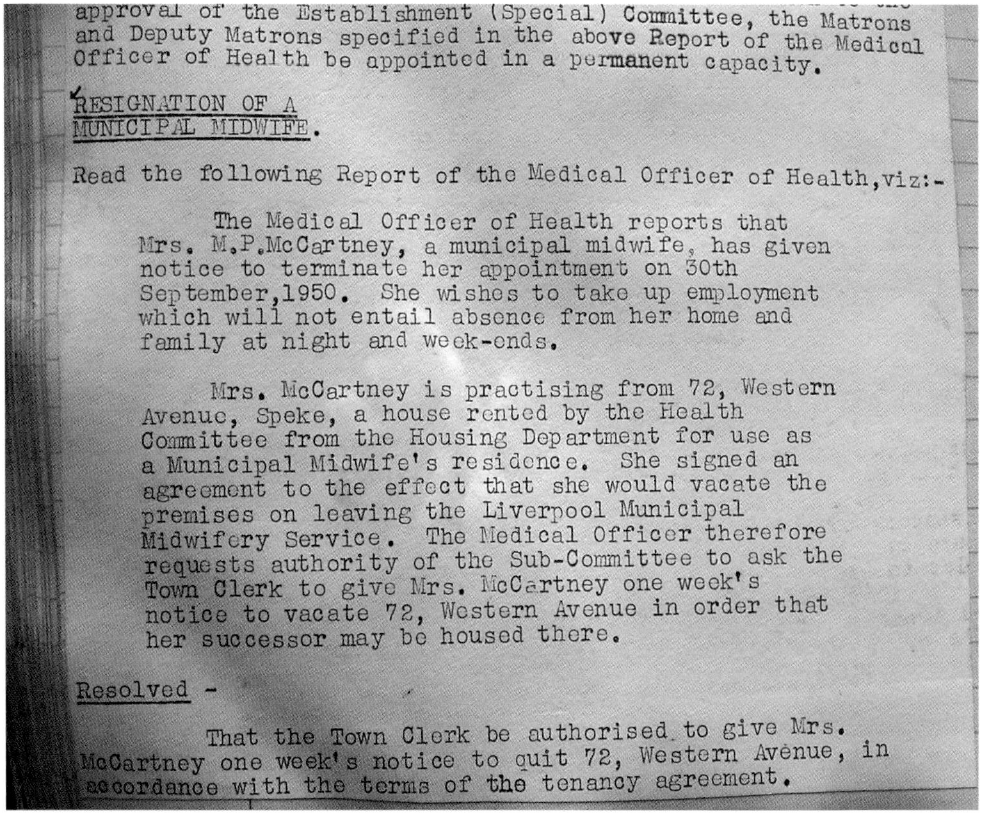

approval of the Establishment (Special) Committee, the Matrons and Deputy Matrons specified in the above Report of the Medical Officer of Health be appointed in a permanent capacity.

RESIGNATION OF A
MUNICIPAL MIDWIFE.

Read the following Report of the Medical Officer of Health, viz:-

The Medical Officer of Health reports that Mrs. M.P.McCartney, a municipal midwife, has given notice to terminate her appointment on 30th September, 1950. She wishes to take up employment which will not entail absence from her home and family at night and week-ends.

Mrs. McCartney is practising from 72, Western Avenue, Speke, a house rented by the Health Committee from the Housing Department for use as a Municipal Midwife's residence. She signed an agreement to the effect that she would vacate the premises on leaving the Liverpool Municipal Midwifery Service. The Medical Officer therefore requests authority of the Sub-Committee to ask the Town Clerk to give Mrs. McCartney one week's notice to vacate 72, Western Avenue in order that her successor may be housed there.

Resolved -

That the Town Clerk be authorised to give Mrs. McCartney one week's notice to quit 72, Western Avenue, in accordance with the terms of the tenancy agreement.

The minutes of the health committee meeting when Mary's resignation was accepted, September 1 1950

The McCartneys moved to
12 Ardwick Road after
Mary resigned as a midwife

STOCKTON WOOD
NURSERY
Welcome to
Stockton Wood Primary School
Foundation Stage Entrance
Tel: 0151 486 1778

The redeveloped Stockton
Wood Primary, as it looks today

NEW HOME IN SPEKE

The new home in Ardwick Road was at the other end of the Speke estate from Western Avenue, so there wasn't too much disruption for Paul, aged eight, and Michael, aged six, as they were still living in the same area and attending the same school. Mary soon got another job, as a health visitor. This was a lot better for her as she could be at home with her family without call-outs in the middle of the night.

The McCartney home was a happy one. Mary was always there for Paul and Michael, making sure the house was warm, clean and cosy, and their meals were always ready for them.

Their mum was also on hand to help with their homework – education was very important to Mary, as she believed Paul and Michael could achieve any goals they set themselves by doing well at school. Mary was there to give them a goodnight kiss before tucking them into their beds, leaving the landing light on so they wouldn't get too scared of the dark.

Jim was the head of the house and very proud of his boys. He was always playing silly jokes on them (the type of jokes only dads normally laugh at) and he also enjoyed taking them on long bike rides, teaching them the ways of the world, letting them finish his crossword and showing them how to use a dictionary if they didn't understand the meaning of words.

SCHOOL DAYS

Paul and Michael enjoyed their childhood but because of the population explosion after the war, Stockton Wood couldn't accommodate every child in the Speke area so many of their pupils were moved to another school. Paul and Michael were both affected and were forced to get a bus to Belle Vale, which was further out in the countryside. Their new school was Joseph Williams County Primary, which opened in 1950.

Although the Jim Mac Band never reformed after the war, Jim would still enjoy playing his piano and trumpet, and just like his father encouraged him to take up an instrument, he would frequently encourage Paul and Michael to play music. The McCartney house was a very musical home, with Mary often whistling while she was doing the housework. It was only a matter of time before the boys would have a go at playing something.

Jim's other passion was gardening, which led to him becoming the secretary of the Speke Horticultural Society. Paul and Michael went around the streets of Speke with their dad, putting posters up in the local shops for Jim's gardening society.

This is where Joseph Williams County Primary school stood. Although it closed in 1997, the road sign was still in place in October 2009. The site is opposite Belle Vale Shopping Centre

LIVERPOOL POST,
OCTOBER 31, 1950

Post. 31-10-50

Young artists busy in their new school

Pupils of the Infants' Department of the Joseph Williams Primary Schoo are busily engaged in their painting following the official opening of thei school by Alderman J. Williams (chairman of Liverpool Educatioı Committee). Watching them are left to right: Mr Leonard William (Alderman Williams' son), Mr H. S. Magnay (director of Education), Alder man J. Williams and Councillor C. E. Booth (chairman of the Primar Education sub-committee).

Newspaper report showing pupils at the official opening of Joseph Williams Primary school in October 1950

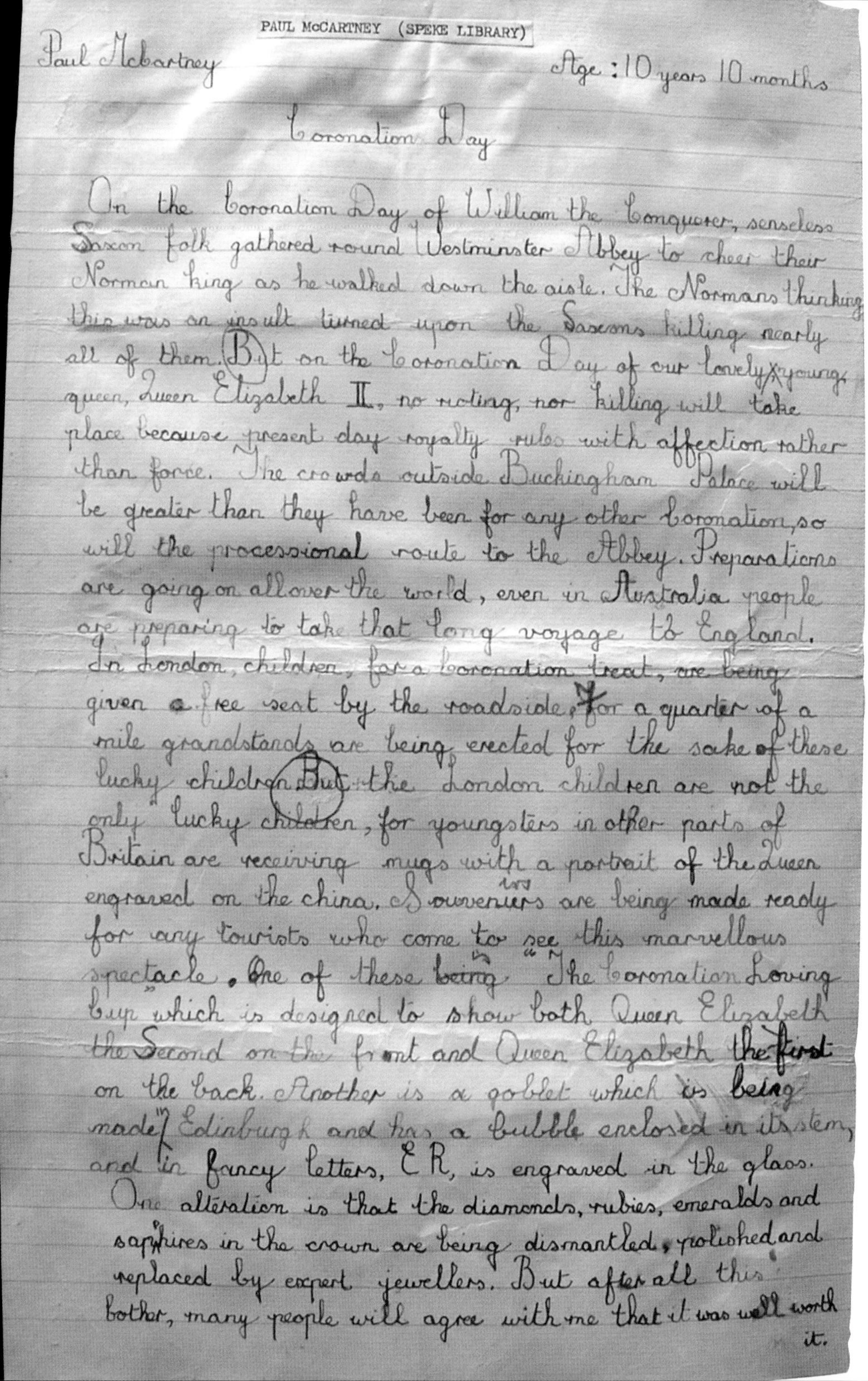

PAUL McCARTNEY (SPEKE LIBRARY)

Paul McCartney   Age: 10 years 10 months

Coronation Day

On the Coronation Day of William the Conqueror, senseless Saxon folk gathered round Westminster Abbey to cheer their Norman king as he walked down the aisle. The Normans thinking this was an insult turned upon the Saxons killing nearly all of them. But on the Coronation Day of our lovely young queen, Queen Elizabeth II, no rioting, nor killing will take place because present day royalty rules with affection rather than force. The crowds outside Buckingham Palace will be greater than they have been for any other Coronation, so will the processional route to the Abbey. Preparations are going on allover the world, even in Australia people are preparing to take that long voyage to England. In London, children, for a Coronation treat, are being given a free seat by the roadside. For a quarter of a mile grandstands are being erected for the sake of these lucky children. But the London children are not the only lucky children, for youngsters in other parts of Britain are receiving mugs with a portrait of the Queen engraved on the china. Souvenirs are being made ready for any tourists who come to see this marvellous spectacle. One of these being "The Coronation Loving Cup" which is designed to show both Queen Elizabeth the Second on the front and Queen Elizabeth the first on the back. Another is a goblet which is being made in Edinburgh and has a bubble enclosed in its stem, and in fancy letters, E R, is engraved in the glass.

One alteration is that the diamonds, rubies, emeralds and sapphires in the crown are being dismantled, polished and replaced by expert jewellers. But after all this bother, many people will agree with me that it was well worth it.

Left: Paul's award-winning essay

Right: A newspaper report of the coronation competition, featuring a complete list of winners

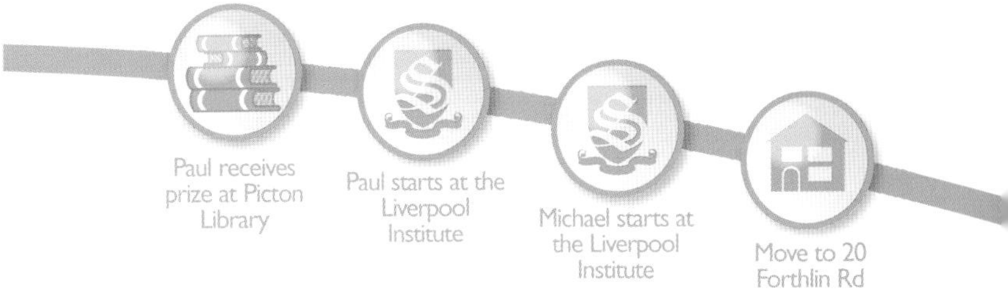

CHAPTER 7

HER MAJESTY'S A PRETTY NICE GIRL

CHILDREN WRITE ON THE CORONATION

Imagination in Essays and Poems

THERE were 509 entries from schoolchildren who are also members of the junior branch libraries, Liverpool Corporation, in the Coronation competition for essays, poems and recitations, organised by the Liverpool Public Libraries, with Mrs. D. Lymer as prime mover.

The standard was so good that Dr. G. Chandler, City Librarian (who told me how much he had enjoyed reading the winning entries) is to have the poems and essays placed in a frame and exhibited in the entrance to the Picton Library.

The essays and poems, he said, show great imagination and not a little skill. So impressed with the entries were many of the 29 Branch librarians, who acted as adjudicators, that they have

By DOROTHY RIMMER

implemented the number of prizes, donating additional prizes themselves.

The Competition was in three parts:—

1. Original composition, either essay or poem;
2. Recitation of suitable poem (adjudicated by branch librarian).
3. Essay or poem written by children under eleven.

Girls far outnumbered the boys in their entries.

The majority of the written entries show a keen knowledge of the Coronation ceremony. Some displayed a vivid imagination such as the child who wrote as a butterfly giving an eye-witness story of the pomp and ceremony at the Abbey.

Several writers expressed sorrow that Queen Mary could not see the Coronation.

Two Brae-street Secondary School pupils — June Weeks and Rita Evans—compiled Coronation booklets, artistically illustrated with coloured pictures as in a scrap-book, with neatly-written details of the story of, in the case of June, the life of Queen Victoria, while Rita's theme was the Crown Jewels.

These two scholars will receive highly-commended prizes.

"A Royal Dream" as dreamed by Queen Elizabeth I, seeing the crowning of Elizabeth II was the imaginative essay told by 11-year-old Jean Whitehead, Tulloch-street, Liverpool, 6.

Eleven-year-old Eileen Moore, Thurlow House, Liverpool, 3, calls her poem "The Ride to the Abbey."

Pomp and gaiety, this is the day.
The procession draws near,
The crowd starts to sway.
Trumpets and drums begin to blare out,
From the end of the road there comes a loud shout,
The Queen. The Queen. Yes it is the Queen,
Erect with emotion and pride,
On to the Abbey she goes with a smile,
With her consort by her side.

Of the Queen, Winifred Cooke, aged nine, Oxenholme-crescent, Liverpool, says:

God grant her peace and happiness,
And strength to rule her people.
The bells will all ring gaily
From big high towers and steeple.

Jeffery R. Morgan, aged eight, Shirley-road, Liverpool, 19, submitted this prize-winning poem:—

The Queen has got a golden crown upon her royal head,
To Westminster Abbey to be crowned, by horses she is led.
The people cheer her on her way while she waves her hand,
And soon our monarch she will be, the Queen to rule our land.
In Westminster Abbey where she's crowned the choirs will joyfully sing.

When the Lord Mayor of Liverpool presents prizes to the 60 scholars in the Picton Hall on May 27, some of the winners in the recitation section will be asked to recite their own poems.

The Prizewinners

A prize was awarded for the best submission from each branch of Liverpool Corporation Public Library.

Appended below is a list of those prizewinners.

SECTION 1. ESSAY OR POEM (Over 11).

Catherine Foster, 107b, Sutton-street, 3; St. Cecilia's.
David Chadwick, 6, Laxton-road, 19; Liverpool Institute.
Jennifer Vaak, 44, Cavan-road, 11; Broad Square.
Irene Stoddart, 36b, Caryl-gardens, 8; St. Patrick's.
John Mellor, 61, Marldon-road, 12; Broad Square.
Hilda Wood, 33, Marmion-road, 17; St. Michael's.
June Weeks, 15, Canova-street, 7; Brae Street.
Pamela Rush, 7, Lovelace-road, 19; Duncombe-road.

Joyce Richards, 12, Manica-crescent; Fazakerley County Primary School.

SECTION 3. ESSAY OR POEM (Under 11).

Paul McCartney, 12, Ardwick-street, Speke; Joseph Williams.
Edward O'Neill, 63, Panton-road, 13; Lister Drive.
Thomas Fitzgerald, 33, Ashfield 15; Hey Green Road.
Sheila Perrin, 33, Wharncliffe-road; St.

PAUL'S ESSAY

Paul's first time on stage was during his final year at Joseph Williams Primary. When he was 11, his school set homework which was a competition run by Liverpool's libraries. The homework was to write an essay or poem about the Queen's coronation. As usual, Paul completed his task and handed it in. Unknown to him, his essay, along with hundreds of others from across the city, was entered into the competition, and it was a proud moment for his mum and dad when the news arrived that Paul had won in his age-group category.

The prize-giving ceremony took place at ***Picton Library*** on William Brown Street, in front of a packed hall, on May 27 1953. When the time came to announce the winner of the under-11s, Paul was trembling with nerves. Then came the words: "And the winner is James Paul McCartney." This was a thrilling but terrifying moment for Paul who had to go onto the stage to collect his well-deserved book token from the Lord Mayor of Liverpool, as well as very moving for his mum and dad.

PAUL MOVES TO SENIOR SCHOOL

Later in 1953 Paul left junior school, to move up to the seniors. Mary and Jim put him forward to the ***Liverpool Institute High School for Boys***, a prestigious boys' grammar school. For Paul to have any sort of a chance of gaining entry into one of Liverpool's leading schools he had to pass the 11-plus exam, so Mary would gently push him to the point were she knew he would succeed. He did pass, making his mum and dad proud again, and his first day at the Institute was on September 9 1953.

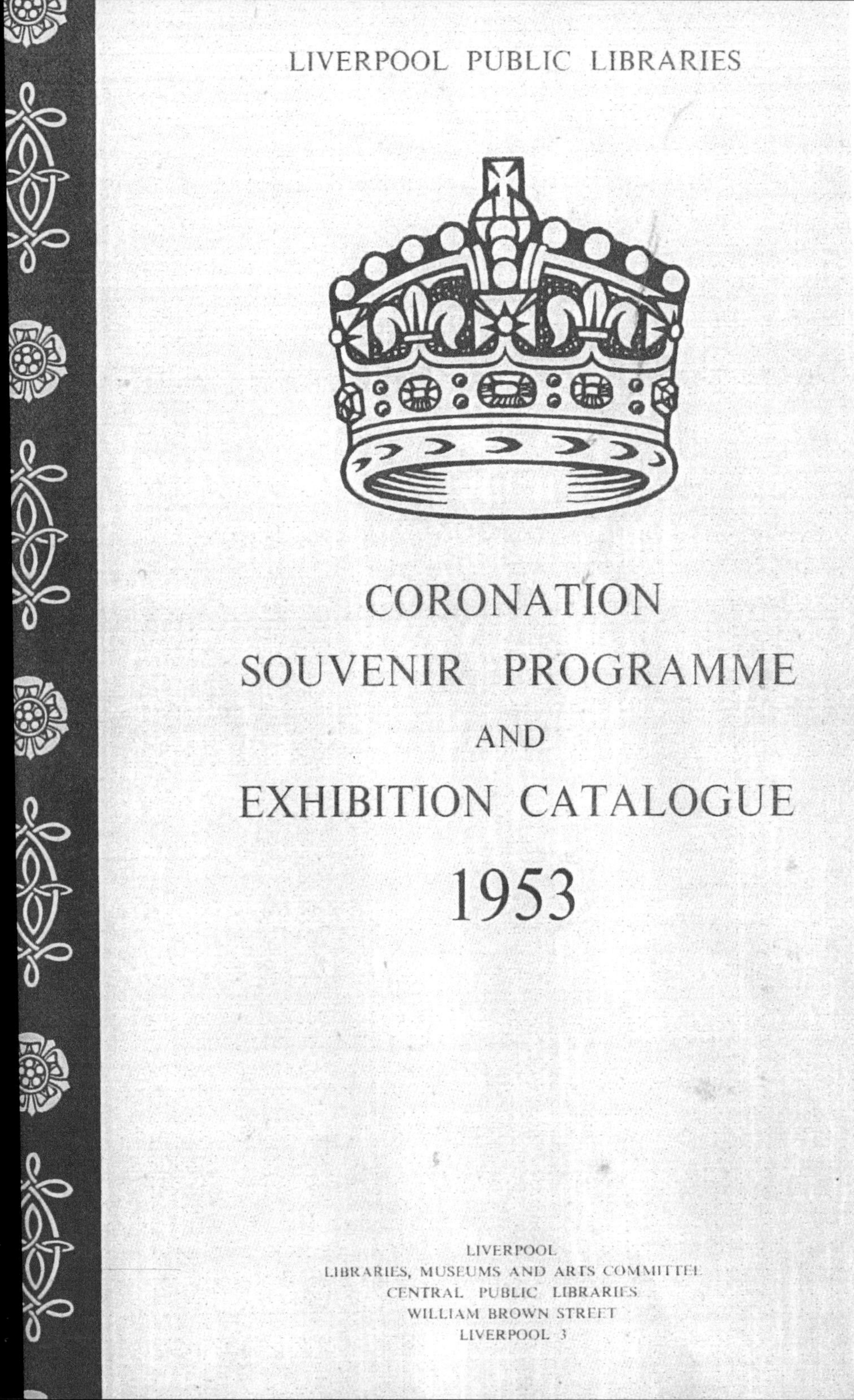
LIVERPOOL PUBLIC LIBRARIES

CORONATION
SOUVENIR PROGRAMME
AND
EXHIBITION CATALOGUE
1953

LIVERPOOL
LIBRARIES, MUSEUMS AND ARTS COMMITTEE
CENTRAL PUBLIC LIBRARIES
WILLIAM BROWN STREET
LIVERPOOL 3

The programme cover for the Liverpool Public Libraries' coronation celebration

LIVERPOOL PUBLIC LIBRARIES

Wednesday, May 6th

at 6.30 p.m. in all the
JUNIOR LIBRARIES

CORONATION COMPETITIONS FOR CHILDREN

Three book prizes will be awarded at each library for essays, poems and recitations about the Coronation or Royalty

1. Original composition, either essay or poem
2. Recitation of suitable poem
3. Essay or poem written by child under eleven

The competition is open to all members of the Junior Libraries. The prizes will, it is hoped, be presented by the Lord Mayor of Liverpool in the Picton Hall at a special film show on 27th May at 7.30 p.m. (see *Page Six*)

ENTRY FORMS, OBTAINABLE FROM ANY BRANCH LIBRARY, MUST BE SENT IN BY 25TH APRIL

Branch	*Postal Address*	*Adjudicator*
Dingle Mount	South Hill Road, 8	Miss P. M. Wardle, A.L.A.
Everton	St. Domingo Road, 5	Miss E. A. Pilling, A.L.A.
Edge Hill	Lodge Lane, 8	J. B. Stephens
Fazakerley	Longmoor Lane, 10	Miss H. Walker, A.L.A.
Garston	Bowden Road, 19	G. Philpott, F.L.A.
Kensington	Kensington, 7	B. Clausson, A.L.A.
Kirkdale	Stanley Road, 5	H. R. Hikins, A.L.A.
Knotty Ash	Dovecot Place, 14	Miss D. G. Dance, F.L.A.
Larkhill	Muirhead Avenue, 13	Miss E. K. Wilson, F.L.A.
Norris Green	Townsend Avenue, 11	F. Hope, A.L.A.
Old Swan	Prescot Road, 13	W. Negus, A.L.A.
Rawdon	Breck Road, 4	H. S. Brown, F.L.A.
Scotland Road	Scotland Road, 5	Miss E. M. Parry, A.L.A.
Sefton Park	Aigburth Road, 17	G. McBride, F.L.A.
Speke	Blackrod Avenue, 19	W. G. Jones, A.L.A.
Toxteth	Windsor Street, 8	Miss G. M. Davies
Walton	Evered Avenue, 9	Miss G. S. Smith, F.L.A.
Wavertree	Picton Road, 15	J. R. Cowan, F.L.A.
West Derby	Green Lane, 13	J. S. Parsonage, F.L.A.
Woolton	Allerton Road, Woolton	Miss L. Baker

LIVERPOOL PUBLIC LIBRARIES

Wednesday, May 27th

at 7.30 p.m. in the

PICTON HALL

PRESENTATION OF PRIZES

(It is hoped that the Lord Mayor of Liverpool will present the prizes)

Chairman: ALDERMAN WALTER CLARK, J.P.
Chairman, Lectures Sub-Committee

FILMS

"HALF CENTURY"

A film which recalls the most interesting events from the funeral of Edward VII to the birth of Prince Charles

"ACROSS CANADA WITH PRINCESS ELIZABETH"

"ROYAL MARRIAGE"

"ROYAL WEDDING PRESENTS"

"ROYAL MOTHERS"

All seats reservable, price 6d.

Children must be accompanied by an adult

Competition rules explained and the order of events for the presentation evening

TRANSCRIPT OF PAUL'S ESSAY

On the Coronation Day of William the Conqueror, senseless Saxon folk gathered round Westminster Abbey to cheer their Norman king as he walked down the aisle. The Normans, thinking this was an insult, turned upon the Saxons, killing nearly all of them.

But on the Coronation Day of our lovely, young queen, Queen Elizabeth II, no rioting nor killing will take place because present day royalty rules with affection rather than force. The crowds outside Buckingham Palace will be greater than they have been for any other Coronation, so will the processional route to the Abbey.

Preparations are going on all over the world, even in Australia people are preparing to take that long voyage to England. In London, children, for a Coronation treat, are being given a free seat by the roadside. For a quarter of a mile grandstands are being erected for the sake of these lucky children. But the London children are not the only lucky children, for youngsters in other parts of Britain are receiving mugs with a portrait of the Queen engraved on the china.

Souvenirs are being made ready for any tourists who come to see this marvellous spectacle. One of these being "The Coronation Loving Cup" which is designed to show both Queen Elizabeth the Second on the front and Queen Elizabeth the First on the back. Another is a goblet which is being made in Edinburgh and has a bubble enclosed in its stem, and, in fancy letters, ER is engraved in the glass.

One alteration is that the diamonds, rubies, emeralds and sapphires in the crown are being dismantled, polished and replaced by expert jewellers. But after all this bother, many people will agree with me that it was well worth it.

The magnificent Picton Library, where Paul received his prize

Mr JR Edwards, the headmaster of the Liverpool Institute when the McCartney boys attended the school

Right and opposite: The Liverpool Institute building, which is now the Liverpool Institute For Performing Arts (LIPA). Its lead patron is Sir Paul McCartney

MOUNT STREET

School register showing 'James Paul McCartney', his date of birth and a change in the family's address

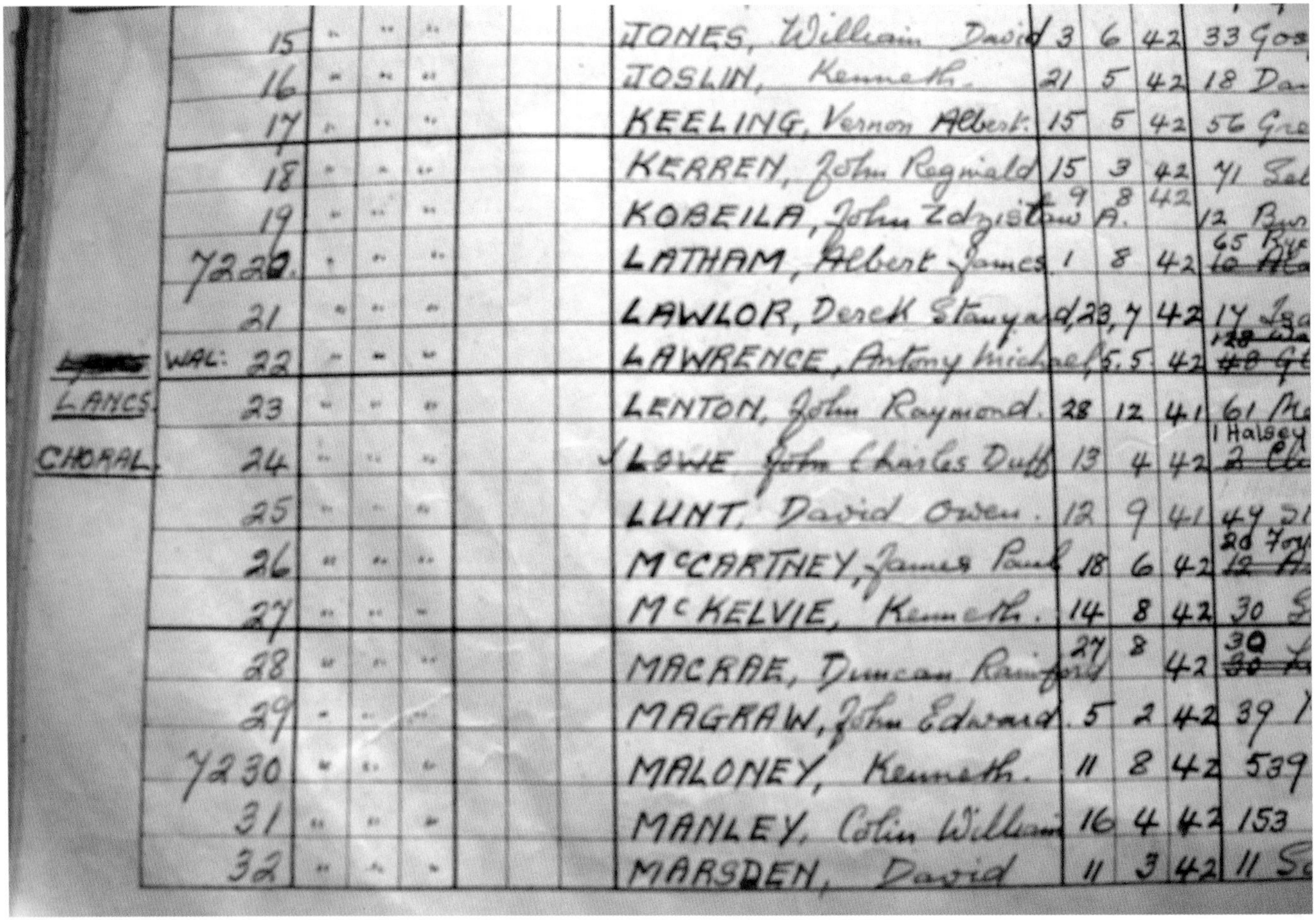

	15	JONES, William David	3	6	42	33 Go…
	16	JOSLIN, Kenneth.	21	5	42	18 Da…
	17	KEELING, Vernon Albert.	15	5	42	56 Gr…
	18	KERREN, John Reginald	15	3	42	71 …
	19	KOBEILA, John Zdzislaw A.	9	8	42	12 Bur…
	7220	LATHAM, Albert James	1	8	42	65 …
	21	LAWLOR, Derek Stanyard	23	7	42	17 …
WAL:	22	LAWRENCE, Antony Michael	5	5	42	~~40 G…~~
LANCS	23	LENTON, John Raymond.	28	12	41	61 …
CHORAL	24	LOWE John Charles Duff	13	4	42	1 Halsey …
	25	LUNT, David Owen.	12	9	41	49 …
	26	McCARTNEY, James Paul	18	6	42	20 For… / ~~12 A…~~
	27	McKELVIE, Kenneth.	14	8	42	30 …
	28	MACRAE, Duncan Rainford	27	8	42	30 …
	29	MAGRAW, John Edward	5	2	42	39 …
	7230	MALONEY, Kenneth.	11	8	42	539
	31	MANLEY, Colin William	16	4	42	153
	32	MARSDEN, David	11	3	42	11 …

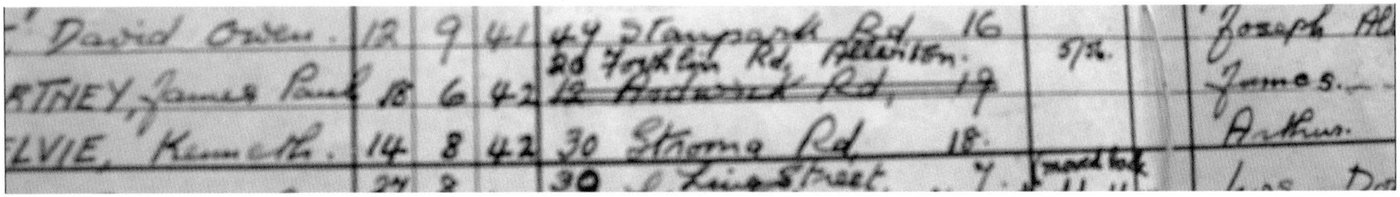

…David Owen.	12	9	41	49 Stampank Rd	16	5/56.	Joseph …
…RTNEY, James Paul	18	6	42	20 Forthlin Rd, Allerton. / ~~12 Ardwick Rd,~~	19		James.
…LVIE, Kenneth.	14	8	42	30 Stroma Rd	18.		Arthur.

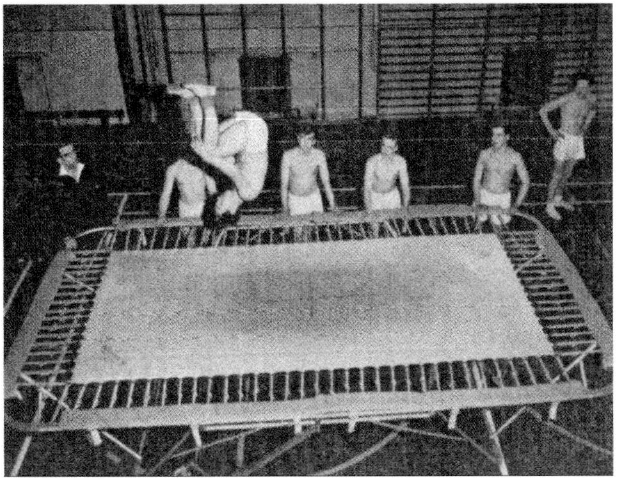

Top left: The photographic darkroom in the Liverpool Institute, 1961

Top right: A smiling Michael after he passed the 11-plus. *Copyright: Michael McCartney*

Above: An acrobatic pupil shows his prowess on the trampoline in the Institute gym, 1961

Now that Paul was settled in his new school, Mary's attention turned to the younger ***Michael, who also wanted to go to the Liverpool Institute***. Michael was different and didn't fit into school life. His early junior school reports describe him as being "a rather silly boy". With this in mind Mary would encourage him to do well so he would also pass the 11-plus. On the day the results came out, he rushed home to his mum, who was preparing tea, and delivered the news: "Mum, I've passed, I'm going to the Institute too." Michael's reward was a great big hug. He started at the Institute on September 7 1955.

McCARTNEYS MOVE TO FORTHLIN ROAD, ALLERTON

In 1955 Paul and Michael were both in senior school, but Mary was still pushing, still wanting to better herself and the family, so it was time for another house move. The family headed to Allerton, to ***20 Forthlin Road***, leaving behind them happy memories of Speke.

During this time, the boys were nagging their dad to teach them the piano. Jim refused but agreed to pay for music lessons. They were deflated with having to learn the basics, as they wanted to play the piano just like their dad. It wasn't long before they both packed in the lessons.

Jim managed to save £15 to buy Paul a trumpet. He tried it out but soon realised it wasn't for him, so his dad gave him permission to swap it for a guitar. Being left-handed, he had to change all the strings over before he could master the basic chords. Meanwhile, Michael was going in a different direction – his interest was photography, so his dad gave him the use of the family camera. He became a regular visitor to the local library, borrowing all the books he could find on photography. He also enjoyed his early years in senior school, taking part in the school sports day – he came second in the high jump.

The police training ground in Allerton, 1953. The rear of the houses in Forthlin Road can be seen in the background

SCHOOL SPORTS

The School Sports Festival was held at Mersey Road on Saturday, 2nd June, on a fine but blustery afternoon. There were intermittent showers, but the threatened depression did not materialise, and the weather was an improvement upon that of last year. Indeed, if any trust may be reposed in weather cycles, the prospects for good conditions in 1957 are extremely promising!

RESULTS

100 Yards—U.12, 1st J. Bloore, 2nd G. M. Day, 3rd D. W. T. Hughes. U.13, 1st P. S. Jones, 2nd D. A. Macauley, 3rd J. Sale. U.14, 1st C. J. Byrne, 2nd G. C. Winslow, 3rd J. F. Griffiths. U.15, 1st S. G. Hill, 2nd J. Winstanley, 3rd J. E. Chapman. U.16, 1st D. G. Langton, 2nd D. W. Todd, 3rd P. G. Daniel. Open, 1st E. Bennett, 2nd J. M. Radcliffe, 3rd G. I. Davies.

220 Yards—U.12, 1st J. R. Davies, 2nd C. R. Blyth, 3rd G. M. Day. U.13, 1st K. A. Jones, 2nd D. A. Macauley, 3rd J. Sale. U.14, 1st C. J. Byrne, 2nd N. T. Egerton, 3rd D. L. Brown. U.15, 1st S. G. Hill, 2nd D. D. Wright, 3rd J. E. Chapman. U.16, 1st D. W. Todd, 2nd D. G. Langton, 3rd P. W. Johnson, 4th J. R. Winnington. Open, 1st E. Bennett, 2nd P. Hallam, 3rd J. M. Radcliffe.

440 Yards—U.13, 1st R. T. Green, 2nd J. Sale, 3rd D. R. Norris. U.15, 1st B. A. Howard, 2nd D. D. Wright, 3rd J. E. Chapman. Open, 1st P. Hallam, 2nd W. F. Morton, 3rd S. G. Norris.

880 Yards—U.15, 1st B. A. Howard. 2nd E. J. Brabins, 3rd P. Cain. Open, 1st V. N. Cowan, 2nd W. F. Morton, 3rd S. G. Norris.

One Mile—U.16, 1st W. J. Rigby, 2nd D. Wilson, 3rd P. A. Dunne. Open 1st V. N. Cowan, 2nd F. D. Welton, 3rd S. G. Norris.

Cricket Ball—U.13, 1st D. W. T. Hughes, 2nd J. Park, 3rd A. Houghton. U.15, 1st V. A. Keeling. 2nd L. W. Harding, 3rd D. N. Holgate.

Long Jump—U.13, 1st P. S. Jones, 2nd W. A. A. Thom, 3rd G. R. Gorst. U.15, 1st M. Pickett, 2nd C. J. Byrne, 3rd J. S. Winstanley. Open, 1st G. I. Davies, 2nd D. G. Langton, 3rd D. W. Todd.

High Jump—U.13, 1st D. A. Macauley, 2nd P. M. McCartney, 3rd A. Houghton. U.15, 1st A. G. Gilbert. 2nd C. J. Byrne, 3rd D. A. Campbell. Open, 1st D. W. Todd, 2nd D. G. Evans, 3rd R. J. Walker.

Results of the Institute sports day held on June 2 1956. Michael came second in the high jump

This is how 20 Forthlin Road looks today. It is now owned by the National Trust, who run guided tours of the former McCartney family home

CLG 832B

CHAPTER 8
LET IT BE

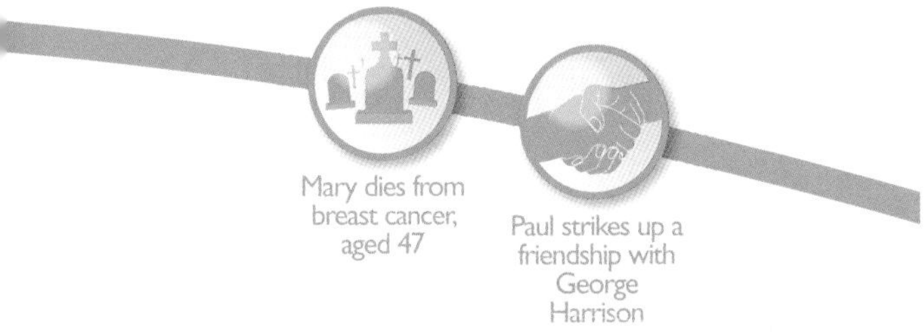

Left: Northern Hospital, Leeds Street, 1968

MARY FALLS ILL

During 1955 Mary started to suffer with chest pains, for which she would treat herself with antacid powder such as Bisodol. Jim was becoming more and more concerned about his wife's health and had made arrangements for a specialist to examine her. Being a qualified nurse, Mary had a good idea what her problem was and the specialist just confirmed it – she was suffering with breast cancer.

The news came as a great blow to Jim. They both decided to try and keep it from their boys, which they achieved until one day in the summer of 1956 when Michael heard his mum weeping in her bedroom, and sheepishly went in to ask what was wrong. She was holding a crucifix and a photo of one of her relatives, who was a Catholic priest. Mary turned to Michael and softly replied: "Nothing love."

Mary had to be admitted into the Northern Hospital for a mastectomy operation. She feared the worst and just wanted to be left alone to come to terms with what was happening. In the weeks leading up to the operation, Jim and Mary had become closer to each other and reflected on their life together, trying to be optimistic. Mary being Mary, she would have told Jim how to look after Paul and Michael, and what her expectations were for them. Jim would reassure her not to worry.

MARY'S DEATH

While Mary was in the Northern Hospital, Paul and Michael went to stay with their uncle Joe and auntie Joan. After the operation, Paul and Michael visited their mum. Jim had explained to them what was going on and that their mum was very ill, but that didn't prepare them for seeing her looking very sick with blood visible on the hospital bed sheets. Sadly for Paul and Michael, that was the last time they saw their mum. The dreaded news came the next morning as soon as they woke up – it was auntie Joan who had to tell them that ***their mum had died. The date was October 31 1956.***

Mary's untimely death at the age of 47 left a terrible void in the lives of those closest to her. Paul, aged 14, and Michael, aged 12, were distraught. The initial shock for Jim was obvious to his brother and sisters, who rallied together to try and console him, while Paul and Michael were staying with their uncle and auntie. Mary's funeral took place on November 3 at St Bernadettes Church, Mather Avenue, Allerton, close to the family home on Forthlin Road. Mary kept her Catholic faith to the end and was buried fortified with the rites of the Holy Church and with her rosary beads around her wrist.

LIFE WITHOUT MUM

After the funeral, Jim was left to try and bring up the two young boys as Mary would have expected. The extended family of aunties and uncles pulled together to help him, taking it in turns to pop into Forthlin Road to help with the cleaning and the cooking, while making a traditional Sunday roast dinner on a Monday night.

A few days after the funeral, Paul found himself at a concert at the Liverpool Empire, watching Lonnie Donegan and his skiffle group. For those few hours he was lost in a world of rock 'n' roll. After the concert Paul returned home and picked up his guitar. He found comfort in playing it.

Michael was haunted with nightmares of life without his beloved mum. For him the house was an empty shell without her there. Although there were many visitors to Forthlin Road, for Michael the home didn't have a heart any more – his mum was his life, his best friend and she had been taken from him. He turned more to photography, making Paul his main subject, but for him life would never be the same again.

On returning to school, which involved a long journey on the 86 bus down Allerton Road and past Penny Lane, Paul befriended another Institute boy after picking him out because of the school uniform. His name was George Harrison, who lived in Speke at 25 Upton Green, which was only a few streets away from Paul's old address of Ardwick Road. Paul was to become a very close friend to George because he was also into rock 'n' roll and played the guitar. Although George was a year below Paul at school, the age difference didn't matter – what was more important was their common interest.

St Bernadettes RC Church, Mather Avenue, where a requiem mass was held for Mary

Paul strums on his guitar in the back garden of Forthlin Road, shortly after Mary died. This photo was taken by his brother

86
PIER HEAD
ALLERTON
SMITHDOWN RD.
CHURCH ST.
A19
NKD 519

Far left: The 86 bus, 1956. This was the bus that Paul and Michael would take to school and on which Paul was to meet George Harrison

Left: In 2009 the 86 bus continued to follow an almost identical route. Here it is on Allerton Road, approaching the Penny Lane junction

Looking towards the junction of Allerton Road, Smithdown Road and Penny Lane in 1956. On the opposite page is the same perspective 53 years on. The tram lines have disappeared and the area now teems with cars but most of the buildings remain, although the bus shelter is currently derelict

ARBERS
BARBERS
Parkgate
City of Liverpool
PENNY
LANE L18

THE CHURCH OF ENGLAND
THE PARISH OF
ST. PETER, WOOLTON
DIOCESE OF LIVER
SUNDAY SERVICES
8.00am
Holy Communion
Holy Communion (1st & 5th Sundays)
"All Age" Worship (some 2nd Sundays)
"Healing" Service
RECTOR:

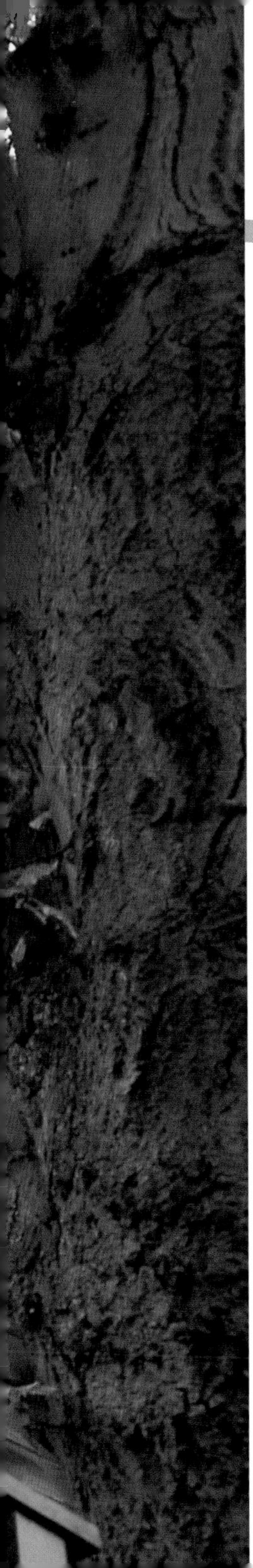

CHAPTER 9 ALL TOGETHER NOW

PAUL WRITES A SONG AND MEETS JOHN LENNON

It was only a few months after his mum's death when Paul wrote his first song, which was called 'I've Lost My Little Girl'. He was only 14 years old.

A friend of Paul's from the Liverpool Institute, Ivan Vaughan, knew of his interest in rock 'n' roll and invited him to a village fete that was being held in the grounds of St Peter's Church, Woolton. The reason for the invitation was for Paul to meet a friend of Ivan's who was starting a skiffle group called the Quarrymen. Paul saw this as an audition and started to practise the songs he was listening to on Radio Luxembourg.

On the day of the fete, July 6 1957, Paul arrived with his guitar and the Quarrymen were already on stage. After their set ***Paul was introduced to the lead singer, John Lennon***. He was older than Paul by almost two years and lived in nearby Menlove Avenue. John asked the then 15-year-old Paul to show him what songs he knew so he started to play the hits of Little Richard, Chuck Berry and Eddie Cochran's 'Twenty Flight Rock'. John was impressed and the two of them retired to a local café to talk about music. A few days after the meeting with Lennon, Ivan told Paul that John would like him to join the Quarrymen. Paul was delighted.

GEORGE HARRISON JOINS THE QUARRYMEN

Shortly after Paul joined the group he wanted his friend George Harrison to also become a member. The problem was his, age, 14, but Paul insisted that a reluctant John listen to George play his guitar. On doing so, John realised that he was naturally talented and could also play lead guitar. A few months passed, George turned 15 and then he joined the Quarrymen. With

Left: St Peter's Church, Woolton, in 2009. This was where Paul McCartney met John Lennon

George now in the group the range of songs they could play expanded because of his talent. It wasn't long before Paul and John started to write their own songs. They struggled to find somewhere to rehearse so Paul's dad stepped in and let them use Forthlin Road.

There were two reasons why Jim agreed to let them rehearse in his home. From his own experience of being in a band, he knew of the need to practice. The second reason was that he didn't really trust the older John Lennon and thought he might be a bad influence on Paul, now the Quarrymen were starting to get bookings around Liverpool.

Although the group was taking up a lot of his time, Paul never let his school work slip, and this was proved on December 15 1959 when he attended the Liverpool Institute's Speech Day, which was held at the Philharmonic Hall. Paul was presented with a special prize for art.

Lord Leverhulme gave a speech warning the boys not to be influenced by what was being reported in certain newspapers about football and rock 'n' roll. He suggested they should aim for a career in industry, citing the need for scientists.

PAUL APPEARS IN LIVERPOOL INSTITUTE PLAY

Paul still had another year left in school, and in his final year, 1960, he took part in the Institute production of 'Saint Joan', playing an assessor. The play ran for seven performances from February 16-20. Another Institute pupil, future ITN and BBC newsreader Peter Sissons, had a leading role as Richard Beauchamp, Earl of Warwick. ***Paul left the Institute on July 21 1960*** with good exam results but was determined that his future lay in music.

Allan Williams, who owned the Jacaranda club on Slater Street, in Liverpool city centre, now managed the Quarrymen. Williams had booked them a two-month contract in Hamburg, Germany. Before Paul could go he had to get permission off his dad, so enlisted the help of his younger brother, Michael.

A NAME CHANGE AND HEADING TO HAMBURG

Jim was reluctant to give his consent but after pressure from Paul, Michael and Allan Williams, who promised to drive Paul and the rest of the group to Hamburg and pay them £2.50 per day, per man (more than Jim was earning), he set aside his worries and gave consent for his son to go with the group.

The Quarrymen were now known as The Silver Beetles with the line-up of: Paul (guitar and vocals), John Lennon (guitar and vocals), George Harrison (guitar and vocals), Stuart Sutcliffe, (an art school friend of John's on bass guitar) and Pete Best (drums). Best was a short notice stand-in who had worked with the group before at the Casbah in Heymans Green, West Derby – a club run by Pete's mum. Between 1960 and 1962, ***The Silver Beetles would divide their time between working in Hamburg and Liverpool***.

PAUL'S OTHER JOBS

While travelling between England and Germany, Paul also tried his hand at doing 'proper' work, helping the delivery driver for Lewis's, one of Liverpool's best shops. This didn't last very long, and then he got a job at Massey and Coggins, an electrical engineering and winding specialist. He started sweeping up before being promoted to the shop floor, winding cogs. He left this job in March 1961. By April 1961 Paul was back in Hamburg, working at the Top Ten Club. It was at this time that the group parted company with their first manager, Allan Williams. It was left to Stuart Sutcliffe, who was no longer a member of the group and living permanently in Hamburg, to inform Williams, which he did by letter.

Michael was in his final year of school when Paul was working at the Top Ten Club. When he left the Liverpool Institute on July 20

GARDEN FETE

ST. PETER'S CHURCH FIELD

WOOLTON PARISH CHURCH Rector: M. Pryce Jones.

Saturday, 6th July, 1957

at 3 p.m.

ADMISSION BY PROGRAMME:

CHILDREN 3d.

PROCEEDS IN AID OF CHURCH FUNDS.

PROGRAMME

STALLS — SIDESHOWS — ICE CREAM — LEMONADE

Teas and Refreshments in large Marquee situated behind the hut.

2-00 p.m. PROCESSION leaves Church Road, via Allerton Road, Kings Drive, Hunt's Cross Avenue; returning to the Church Field.
Led by the Band of the Cheshire Yeomanry.
Street Collection by the Youth Club during the procession.

3-00 p.m. CROWNING OF THE ROSE QUEEN (Miss Sally Wright) by Mrs. Thelwall Jones.

3-10 p.m. FANCY DRESS PARADE.
Class 1. Under 7 years.
Class 2. 7 to 12 years.
Class 3. Over 12 years.
Entrants to report to Miss P. Fuller at the Church Hall before the procession.

3-30 p.m. to 5-00 p.m. MUSICAL SELECTIONS by the Band of the Cheshire (Earl of Chester) Yeomanry. Band-master: H. Abraham.
(By permission of Lt.-Col. G. C. V. Churton, M.C., M.B.E.).

4-15 p.m. THE QUARRY MEN SKIFFLE GROUP.

5-15 p.m. DISPLAY by the City of Liverpool Police Dogs. By kind permission of the Chief Constable and Watch Committee.

5-45 p.m. THE QUARRY MEN SKIFFLE GROUP.

8-0 p.m. GRAND DANCE in the CHURCH HALL

GEORGE EDWARDS BAND also *The Quarry Men Skiffle Group*

TICKETS 2/-

REFRESHMENTS AT MODERATE PRICES.

Above: St Peter's garden fete programme front cover and order of events

Above: John Lennon on stage with the Quarrymen at St Peter's Church fete, on the day he and Paul met

Above: Paul joins John for his first public performance with the Quarrymen, at Norris Green Conservative Club

THE CITY OF LIVERPOOL

LIVERPOOL INSTITUTE HIGH SCHOOL

SPEECH DAY

TUESDAY, DECEMBER 15th, 1959

The PRIZES will be Distributed
and the ADDRESS given by

THE RIGHT HONOURABLE
THE VISCOUNT LEVERHULME, T.D., B.A., J.P.

Chairman: Professor R. A. MORTON, Ph.D., D.Sc., F.R.I.C., F.R.S.

LIVERPOOL INSTITUTE
MDCCCXXV

FOUNDATION PRIZES

The Lord Derby Prizes:	
Mathematics	D. J. Whittaker
Chemistry	A. M. Zalin
French	M. F. McNaughton
German	J. R. P. McKenzie
William Durning Holt Prizes:	
English Essay	J. D. Lunt
Latin	R. T. Crofts
Physics	J. R. Conder
Samuel Booth Prizes:	
English Literature	D. Reed
Greek	R. T. Crofts
F. S. Milliken Prize for History	L. Bivon
Arthur Damsell Prizes for Arithmetic: Senior	A. J. Cowan
Junior	D. H. Mawdsley
Sir Frederick Radcliffe Prizes for Elocution: Senior	R. S. Pybus
Junior	B. R. West
George Herbert Allen Prize for British Commonwealth History	D. S. Rudnick
Agnes Lunt Prize for Lower Sixths	G. I. Davies
Kenneth Boswell Prize for Public Service	J. M. Radcliffe
Sir Donald MacAlister Prize for Public Service	R. T. Crofts W. J. Rigby

SPECIAL PRIZES

Prize for Music	D. Norris
Prize for Spanish	J. D. Lunt
Prize for Latin and Greek Verses—given by Mr. Bentliff	R. T. Crofts
Prize for Art	J. P. McCartney
Prize for French—given by the French Consul	F. J. McKie

Above: Paul (circled) in a Liverpool Institute school photo

Left: Speech Day programme cover and list of prize winners, featuring a\ reference to 'JP McCartney'

Saint Joan school play front cover, title page and cast list

THE LIVERPOOL INSTITUTE Headmaster: J. R. Edwards, M.A.

Presents

'SAINT JOAN'

By BERNARD SHAW

AT 7 P.M. ON

WEDNESDAY, THURSDAY, FRIDAY and SATURDAY,
FEBRUARY 17-20th 1960

AND ON

TUESDAY and WEDNESDAY, FEBRUARY 16th and 17th
AT 2 P.M.

'SAINT JOAN' by Bernard Shaw

CAST (in order of appearance)

ROBERT DE BAUDRICOURT	DAVID WRIGHT
STEWARD	RAYMOND IRLAM
JOAN	LACHLAN MACRAE
BERTRAND DE POULENGY	RODNEY OTHEN
ARCHBISHOP OF RHEIMS	STEPHEN HARLOW
MGR. DE LA TRÉMOUILLE	GRAHAME SETTLE
COURT PAGE	JOHN CUTHELL
GILLES DE RAIS	BRIAN WILSON
CAPTAIN LA HIRE	ALAN BREEZE
THE DAUPHIN (later Charles VII)	JEFFERY MORGAN
DUCHESS DE LA TRÉMOUILLE	BRIAN WEST
DUNOIS, BASTARD OF ORLEANS	MALCOLM BROWN
DUNOIS' PAGE	RAYMOND PHILLIPS
RICHARD DE BEAUCHAMP, EARL OF WARWICK	PETER SISSONS
CHAPLAIN DE STOGUMBER	PATRICK RADCLIFFE
WARWICK'S PAGE	STEVEN NORRIS
PETER CAUCHON, BISHOP OF BEAUVAIS	HOWARD PAUL
THE INQUISITOR	ANTHONY ZALIN
D'ESTIVET	DAVID WILLIAMS
DE COURCELLES	IAN ROBERTSON
BROTHER MARTIN LADVENU	PHILIP JELF
EXECUTIONER	DAVID JONES

ASSESSORS: Brian Parkinson, Iain Taylor, James Woods, Paul McCartney, David Moore, Leslie Trow, Alan Jones, Paul Nener, Andrew Wallard, Geoffrey Latham, Robert Nelson.

COURTIERS: Michael Pearson, Anthony Archer, John Maclean, Terence Quinn, Norman Brooks, George Meadows, Kenneth Martin, David Kelly, Paul Winckles, Leonard Rawlinson, Joseph Capek.

SOLDIERS: Peter Marks, Paul Ellison, Reginald Blyth, David Norris.

THE PLAY PRODUCED BY MR. ALAN DURBAND

1961 he went to stay with his cousin, Bett, and her husband, Mike, at their pub, The Bow Bars in Ryde on the Isle of Wight. Michael worked as a cook and sold hamburgers. On his return home he went to enrol at Liverpool Art College but the education authority had just changed the grading for students and he didn't have enough GCEs to gain entry. His dreams had been shattered and he found himself aged 17 with no school, no college and no job. He was left with no option but to join the dole queue. It wasn't long before Michael found himself employment at Jackson's the tailors, on Ranelagh Street in the city centre.

BACK IN LIVERPOOL

By the end of 1961 Paul and the group were back in Liverpool. They were now known as The Beatles (with an 'a'). The line up was: Paul (guitar and vocals), John Lennon (guitar and vocals), George Harrison (guitar and vocals) and Pete Best (drums). ***The Beatles had a regular session at the Cavern Club in Mathew Street,*** performing at lunchtimes. They had quickly established themselves as one of Liverpool's top groups.

One of the problems facing Paul and John at the Cavern was the groups that went on before them had already played the most popular rock 'n' roll classics. As a result, the Beatles started to play obscure 'B' sides and more of their own stuff. The fans at the Cavern loved it. All the attention they were getting soon reached the Mersey Beat (a music paper sold around Liverpool) who put them on the front cover. This was noticed by Brian Epstein, whose family owned a chain of record shops called NEMS. Brian ran two stores in the city centre, one in Whitechapel and the other in Great Charlotte Street.

Brian decided to go to the Cavern to see what all the fuss was about. When he saw them on stage he was very impressed and realised the potential of the group. He wanted to manage them and approached John and Paul with his offer. They said: "Yeah, okay", but Epstein still had to see Paul's dad.

Jim had known Brian Epstein's father, Harry, and had bought a

Michael with his camera. He was the first Beatles' official/unofficial photographer, capturing the beginning of it all

Lewis's as it stands today

The 1881 census shows that Joe McCartney was working as a barber, aged 14. Eighty years later his grandson, Michael, got a job at a hairdressers

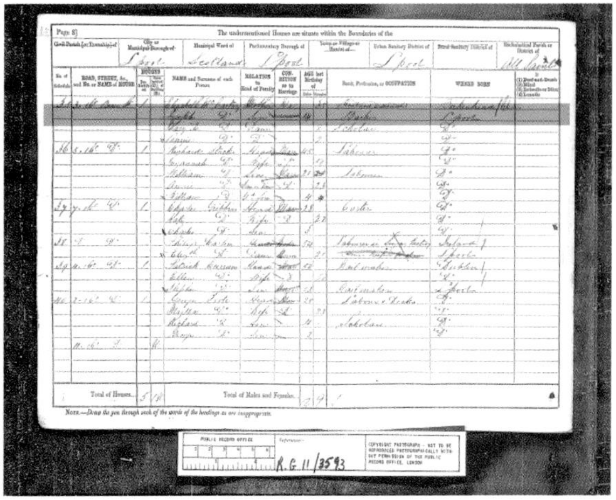

second-hand piano from him after the First World War. With that in mind, Jim trusted the Epstein family, and so it was that Brian Epstein became the Beatles' manager for 25% of their earnings.

MICHAEL CHANGES JOBS

Moving into 1962, Michael had left Jackson's the tailors and started selling Catholic bibles door to door. He sold only one, to his next-door neighbour Mr Gore, and this arrangement lasted for just one week. He moved into the hairdressing business by getting a job at Andre Bernard, on the corner of Great Charlotte Street and Ranelagh Street – just up the road from the tailors. Andre Bernard's was next door to Blacklers department store where George Harrison was working as an apprentice electrician, so it was handy for a quick chat and a cup of tea.

THE BEATLES' FIRST RECORD DEAL AND A NEW DRUMMER

One of the first things Epstein did as manager was to change their image from leather-clad rockers to a more clean-cut, boy-next-door look. He told them to wear suits and also introduced what was to become the trademark Beatles bow, which concluded every gig.

Epstein's trips to London in search of a record deal finally paid off in May 1962. ***George Martin, the head of Parlophone Records, offered the Beatles a contract.*** When they arrived in London to start recording, Martin was pleased with the results, offered them a song and told them it would be a number one. The song was titled 'How Do You Do It'. Paul and John rejected it and wanted the debut single to be their own composition, 'Love Me Do'.

Martin decided that if it was to be their debut release, he wanted to try it with John playing harmonica, to which everyone agreed. Martin also wanted to change the drummer, Pete Best, who had been with the group since the Casbah and Hamburg.

With Best gone the Beatles needed a replacement. The obvious choice was Richard Starkey, who was better known as Ringo

Left: Andre Bernard hairdressers, Great Charlotte Street, 1962, where Michael worked

Below: NEMS record shop on Great Charlotte Street, 1961

Paul performing at the Cavern with the Beatles. The young woman sitting down is Bernadette Byrne (maiden name Farrell). She was George Harrison's girlfriend for a time and went on to co-found The Beatles Story museum in Liverpool

Starr. Ringo was one of Liverpool's top drummers and had worked with the Beatles before in Hamburg and Liverpool while performing in his own group, Rory Storm and the Hurricanes. Epstein phoned Ringo and offered him the job, which he accepted, even though he was to get a lot of abuse from the Pete Best fans back in Liverpool.

The new and final line-up for the Beatles was:
Paul (guitar and vocals), John Lennon (guitar and vocals) George Harrison (guitar and vocals) and Ringo Starr (drums).

It was about this time, while Paul was in London, that things started to happen for Michael in Liverpool. A work friend at the hairdressers, Mike Wineblatt, knew of his interest in the arts, and invited him to meet a few friends of his who were organising the Merseyside Arts Festival. Michael accepted the invitation and was taken to Hope Hall (prior to it becoming the Everyman Theatre), where he was introduced to John Gorman, Roger McGough and the rest of the organisers.

He was completely into what the arts festival was all about: poetry reading, folk singing, comedy sketches and art exhibitions. Gorman and McGough asked Michael if he wanted to take part in a comedy sketch, to which he replied: "I don't do that sort of thing." When asked why not, he said: "I don't know how to." McGough replied: "Neither do we, we just read the script." Michael took part in the sketch and found that he enjoyed performing in front of an audience.

THE FIRST SINGLE

Back in London, Paul and the Beatles had finished recording 'Love Me Do' and on October 5 1962 their debut single was released. On the B-side was one of Paul's own songs called 'PS I Love You'. Although it reached number one in the Liverpool charts, nationally it only made it to 17. What was more important than the chart position was that it launched the Beatles to the nation.

Michael was more and more aware of the McCartney name and he was becoming known as the younger brother of one of the Beatles. At first he accepted the tag, but he was soon to find it a hindrance. He wanted to be known in his own right. This came to a head when it was time to print the programmes for the Merseyside Arts Festival, for which Michael had put in all his spare time and effort.

John Gorman asked him how he wanted his name to appear in the programme. Michael just said: "Put it blank." When the programme was finally printed he had forgotten about his request and was very upset that his name wasn't included. Then he remembered what he said to Gorman, and sure enough his name was there just as he wanted it: 'Michael Blank'.

HOPE HALL
TO BE SOLD

MERSEYSIDE ARTS FESTIVAL

Organisers :

JOHN GORMAN, *Hon. Sec.*

JOHN SEDDON	Mr. LYNSAY
ROGER McGOUGH	IAN PACKER
MICHAEL WEINBLATT	JOHN SHEPHERD
ARTHUR DOOLEY	MICHAEL BLANK
CHENISTON ROLAND	MAVIS PARRY
FRANK McGONIGAL	JULLIE PARRY
Mr. GRANT	ROSALIND

Above: The programme for the 1962 Merseyside Arts Festival, showing Michael's name as 'Michael Blank'

Left: Hope Hall, 1962, on Hope Street. It was here that Michael met Roger McGough and John Gorman

MERSEYSIDE TOP 10, OCTOBER 1962:

1 Love Me Do The Beatles
2 Telstar The Tornadoes
3 The Locomotion Little Eva
4 It Might As Well Rain Until September Carole King
5 Sheila Tommy Roe
6 Ramblin' Rose Nat King Cole
7 She's Not You Elvis Presley
8 Devil Woman Marty Robbins
9 What Now My Love Shirley Bassey
10 You Don't Know Me Ray Charles

UK TOP 20, JANUARY 12 1963:

1 Next Time Cliff Richard
2 Return To Sender Elvis Presley
3 Dance On The Shadows
4 Dance With The Guitar Man Duane Eddy
5 Lovesick Blues Frank Ifield
6 It Only Took a Minute Joe Brown
7 Sun Arise Rolf Harris
8 Go Away Little Girl Mark Wynter
9 Bobby's Girl Susan Maughan
10 Like I Do Maureen Evans
11 Telstar The Tornadoes
12 Up on the Roof Kenny Lynch
13 Telstar The Tornadoes
14 Swiss Maid Del Shannon
15 Desafinado Getz and Charlie Byrd
16 Your Cheating Heart Ray Charles
17 Love Me Do The Beatles
18 A Forever Kind of Love Bobby Vee
19 He's A Rebel The Crystals
20 The Main Attraction Pat Boone

The Beatles' appearance on 'The Ed Sullivan Show' in February 1964 ensured they 'broke' America. Over 70 million people are believed to have watched their debut performance on the show. It was a defining moment

CHAPTER 10
THANK U VERY MUCH

In 1962 Paul took his first steps to international stardom. After five years of touring (1957-1962) the clubs and dance halls of the North West of England and Hamburg, the Beatles had made it.

Paul's level of success as a singer-songwriter was unprecedented and remains unmatched. He has written or co-written over 50 top 10 singles during a career that spans almost half a century.

After the Beatles, Paul continued songwriting and performing with his own group, Wings, before a solo career commenced in 1980. He has picked up countless accolades and awards along the way, one of which was being granted the freedom of the city of Liverpool in 1984.

Michael adopted the professional name of Mike McGear and, with John Gorman and Roger McGough, formed a comedy-music-poetry group, 'The Scaffold'. He has always looked at the funny side of life, and this came through in the records The Scaffold released between 1967 and 1974. Their hits included 'Liverpool Lou', 'Gin Gan Goolie', 'Lily The Pink' and 'Thank U Very Much'.

Michael has also achieved his ambition of becoming an artist, having his photographs commissioned by the National Museums and Galleries. He was there at the beginning of the Beatles, using the family's Kodak Box Brownie camera and then a Rollei Magic

Box, capturing precious images of the group that shook the world. His early photos have been exhibited in galleries around the world, including New York, Los Angeles, Tokyo, London and Liverpool. He has also become an author and his book 'Remember' contains some of those pictures.

The McCartney brothers are proud of their Liverpool roots. Michael and the rest of the family still live in and around the Merseyside area, while Paul visits the city publicly and privately as often as he can.

Their dad, Jim, left Forthlin Road in 1964, after the pressure of the fans camping outside the house made it impossible for him to continue living there. He moved back to Wirral, where the family briefly lived during the war.

Jim was very proud of Paul and Michael and supported them both in their chosen careers. He always showed faith in his boys, and encouraged them to do well. It was the way Paul and Michael were brought up by their mum and dad that drove them to success.

In later years Jim went on to re-marry and gained a stepdaughter, Ruth. After many happy years Jim's health started to deteriorate as he suffered from arthritis. He died on March 18 1976, aged 73. Just before Jim died, he said to his wife Angela: "I'll be with Mary soon."

FAMILY NOTICES

Liverpool Daily Post, March 1976

McCartney March 18th 1976
Peacefully at home, 20 Beverley Drive, Gayton, Wirral. James McCartney, beloved husband of Angela and dear father of Paul, Michael and Ruth.
Private service in his residence, Monday 22nd March followed by cremation at Landican at 10.30am. No flowers please, but donations may be sent for Arthritis research to Leasowe Hospital, Wirral.

Liverpool Echo, November 1956

McCartney October 31st 1956
Suddenly in hospital. Mary McCartney, SRN S.C.M. The dearly loved wife of James, very devoted mother of Paul and Michael (Fortified with rites of Holy Church RIP) Requiem mass at the church of St Bernadette on Saturday next at 9.00am followed by interment at Yew Tree Cemetery – 20 Forthlin Road, Liverpool L8.

McCartney - Mary Patricia
Dearly loved sister of Wilf and Bill, also sister-in-law of Madge and Dilys, sadly missed by all (on whose soul sweet Jesus have mercy) Voelas St.

James McCartney
July 7 1902 – March 18 1976

Mary Patricia McCartney
September 29 1909 – October 31 1956

Everyone's life is important because it touches so many other lives

CHAPTER 11
DO YOU REMEMBER?

The Scaffo[...] about in S[...] Park, Live[...]

Above and left: Liverpool goes wild as The Beatles arrive home in July 1964

Below: Paul performs at the Kings Dock in 1990

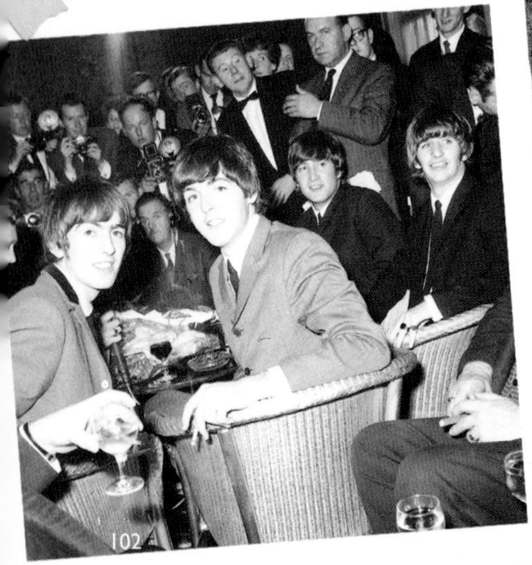

In concert at the Liverpool Empire, 1973

Above: Paul holds court during an interview before the northern premiere of 'A Hard Day's Night'

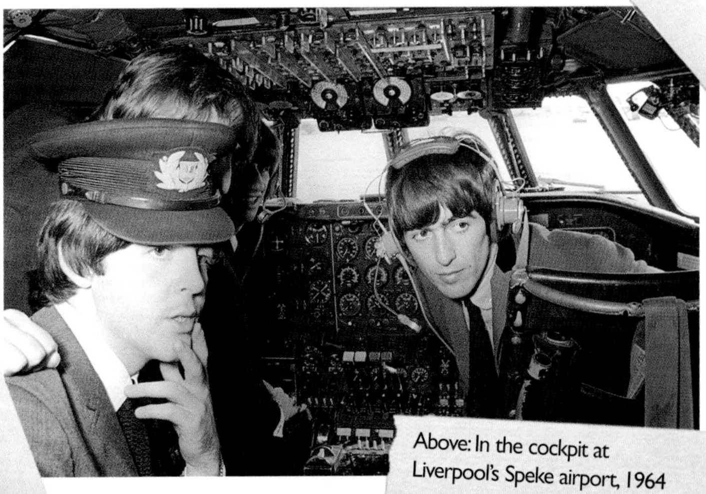

Above: In the cockpit at Liverpool's Speke airport, 1964

Below: A 'Top of the Pops' appearance

The newly-knighted Sir Paul McCartney in 1997

Fooling around backstage at the Liverpool Empire

Paul outside his home in St John's Wood, London, June 1967

Left: In the Abbey Road studios in June 1967 for the famous 'Our World' broadcast

Right: With his adoring public in Liverpool city centre, prior to a book signing, 2001

An historic gig at the Cavern, December 1999

Below: Inside Liverpool's Anglican Cathedral

Michael with one of his acclaimed books of photographs

An aerial view of Paul's Kings Dock concert in 2003. This site is now home to the Echo Arena

The George Harrison tribute concert at the Royal Albert Hall, London, in November 2002

Above right: Paul, Yoko Ono and Olivia Harrison prior to a Stella McCartney fashion show at LIPA. Michael's wife, Ro, is sat immediately behind them

Above: The Scaffold reunite

Celebrating 10 years of the Liverpool Institute For Performing Arts (LIPA)

Above: Michael with an old photograph of himself, Roger McGough and John Gorman

Left: Paul on stage at the Liverpool Sound concert, June 2008

Right: Michael looks across the Mersey with the Liver building in the background

Opposite: Back in the city where it all began, at Anfield, June 2008

Trinity Mirror NW²

Other publications available from Trinity Mirror NW²:

Bigger than the Beatles

Yesterday wasn't just about the Fab Four.
The story of the city's musical odyssey
Free p&p (UK)

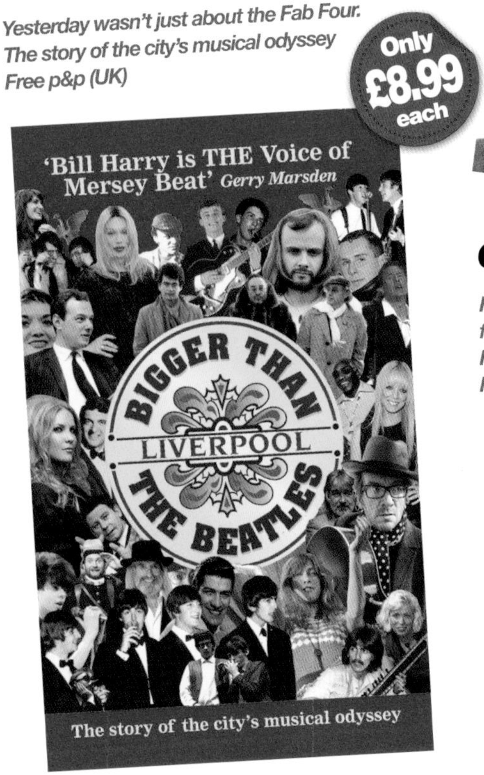

Charlie Landsborough

From Birkenhead teacher to world famous country music star.
Read Charlie's inspirational story
Free p&p (UK)

Dummy Bullets

The story of how one man went to war – with a ventriloquist's dummy
£1.00 p&p (UK)

Trinity Mirror NW²